D0467016

THE SHADOW OF THE EMPIRE

Also by Qiu Xiaolong

The Inspector Chen mysteries

DEATH OF A RED HEROINE
A LOYAL CHARACTER DANCER
WHEN RED IS BLACK
A CASE OF TWO CITIES
RED MANDARIN DRESS
THE MAO CASE
YEARS OF RED DUST (*short story collection*)
DON'T CRY, TAI LAKE
THE ENIGMA OF CHINA
SHANGHAI REDEMPTION
HOLD YOUR BREATH, CHINA *
BECOMING INSPECTOR CHEN *
INSPECTOR CHEN AND THE PRIVATE KITCHEN MURDER *

* *available from Severn House*

THE SHADOW OF THE EMPIRE

Qiu Xiaolong

SEVERN
HOUSE

First world edition published in Great Britain in 2021 and the USA in 2022
by Severn House, an imprint of Canongate Books Ltd,
14 High Street, Edinburgh EH1 1TE.

Trade paperback edition first published in Great Britain and the USA in 2022
by Severn House, an imprint of Canongate Books Ltd.

severnhouse.com

British Library Cataloguing-in-Publication Data
A CIP catalogue record for this title is available from the British Library.

ISBN-13: 978-0-7278-5081-2 (cased)
ISBN-13: 978-1-4483-0739-5 (trade paper)
ISBN-13: 978-1-4483-0738-8 (e-book)

All Severn House titles are printed on acid-free paper.

Typeset by Palimpsest Book Production Ltd.,
Falkirk, Stirlingshire, Scotland.
Printed and bound in Great Britain by
TJ Books, Padstow, Cornwall.

In Memory of Wang Yuanlu

This antique Huizhou writing brush
of scarlet skunk tail came
from Wang Yuanlu. A visiting scholar
of the classical Chinese, too obsessed
with the image of the brush tip
softened on her moist tongue
in Li Shangyin's lines to pound
on the unfeeling computer keyboard,
he went back to China,
asking me to keep the ineffable
touch of a Tang Dynasty brush –
'for inspiration . . .'

‘At his best, man is the noblest of all animals; separated from law and justice he is the worst.’

– Aristotle

‘There are more things in heaven and earth, Horatio,
Than are dreamt of in your philosophy.’

– William Shakespeare

‘Life is like a dream –
I pour out a chalice of wine
To the moon in the river.’

– Su Shi

ONE

'Honorable Judge Dee . . .'

Dee Renjie, the newly appointed Imperial Circuit Supervisor of the Tang Empire, put down the routine report that had been submitted to him earlier in the day, stroking his white-streaked beard and shaking his head reflectively, as if at someone sitting opposite him across the rough, unpainted wooden table in the room of a dilapidated hostel. The hostel was located on the outskirts of Chang'an, the grand capital of the Tang Empire.

Dee was no judge. For the moment, however, he had no objection to people addressing him as such. It sounded far less impressive, further away from the center of the imperial power, though he was in no mood to do anything judge-like whatsoever in the midst of the ferocious political infighting around the throne.

In various official positions during his long, checkered official career, Dee had found himself involved, from time to time, in investigations – even when serving as the prime minister or in other high-ranking official positions. In the Tang system, he had to serve, more often than not, as a multifunctional official with both the executive and judicial powers combined in one position. As he had solved a number of sensitive political cases that had proven to be too difficult for others, people had chosen to simply call him Judge Dee.

In the days of the increasingly fierce power struggle at the imperial court, the title 'judge' had somehow turned into a neutral one, acceptable both to the Wu and the Li factions at the top, he reflected in the trembling candlelight, folding his hands around a cup of lukewarm Dragon Well tea.

The edge of the cup appeared, all of a sudden, to be sharply dented. Rubbing his eyes, he touched it gingerly with his lips in the dimness of the room. He felt so fatigue-laden, not just with the trip that had hardly started but with a lot of other things as well.

For his newly appointed position, Judge Dee had to travel out of the capital to another province, and then still to another. He had left his residence at the center of Chang'an in the morning, and he was now staying incognito for the night at the hostel. The official rank of a circuit supervisor might not have appeared very low to others, but it came as a subtle demotion to him. The Empress Wu had decided to get Judge Dee out of the capital – at least for a short while – with the two factions being engaged in a cut-throat political battle at the pinnacle of power.

Judge Dee had been swept into it because of a memorial he had recently made to the empress, who was debating with herself as to whether her nephew, Internal Minister Wu of the Wu family, or Prince Li, her son with the late emperor of the Li family, would be officially designated as the successor to the throne of the Tang Empire. Like other Confucian scholar-turned-officials, Judge Dee found unacceptable the idea that an imperial concubine-turned-empress would contrive to have someone from the Wu family chosen as the successor for the throne of the Li family, and argued that it was in the time-honored orthodox tradition for the supreme ruler to pick the successor in the son, rather than in the nephew, for the sake of a legitimate, peaceful, and uncontroversial power transition for the empire. While the empress had long regarded Dee as one of the capable, honest officials she could trust, she was nonetheless upset with his bookish argument based on the orthodox Confucian discourse.

To make things worse, the prince happened to have been caught in a scandalous affair with a palace lady. Because of the opposition of old-fashioned officials like Judge Dee, the empress reluctantly agreed not to disown the prince there and then, but she wanted him out of the capital temporarily.

And Judge Dee's new official post entailed his traveling out of Chang'an.

Was that a coincidence?

Lost in thought against the flickering candlelight by the western window of the hostel room, Dee tried not to dwell too much on politics, staring absentmindedly at the blurred reflection of his worn-out self in the bronze mirror.

Again, it started drizzling outside. The small pool in the back of the hostel appeared to be swelling with the memories of those bygone days. A couple of half-forgotten lines were coming back to his mind in the somberness of the room.

A candle trembling against the night rain, / you travel across rivers and lakes, year after year . . .

He would not be able to fall asleep any time soon. It was perhaps just another sign of the onset of old age, he supposed. Still, it appeared to be a quiet and peaceful night, far away from the sordid politics at the imperial court.

Who could tell whether he might come to feel nostalgic, months or years later, about this tranquil moment sitting alone by the hostel window?

He turned back to the reports until a faint drowsiness began creeping over him, suggesting he might finally be ready for bed. Suddenly, out of the darkness, a flash shot swishing through the paper pane of the window, sweeping over in a curve, and striking deep into the old rough wood pillar – just inches from the pile of books on the table he was sitting at – before he could have said or done anything. Surprised, he knocked the teapot from the table as he turned around in a hurry, causing a smashing sound.

Stealthy, hurried footsteps immediately seemed to become audible outside, and then heavy, hurried steps from another direction brought in his long-time attendant/assistant Yang Rong from another hostel room.

'What happened, Master?' Yang said, standing in the doorway, still breathless, barely dressed – he slept naked, a habit formed from his childhood in a poor village of Shandong Province.

As it turned out, the flash had come from a small but sharp knife thrown in from outside and struck into the wooden pillar just above the books on the table – along with a bamboo paper note pinned underneath its pointed tip. It had come within inches of hitting him.

Yang moved to yank out the knife forcefully and spread out the note on the table for Judge Dee.

The note represented a single line written in bold brush strokes.

A high-flying dragon will have something to regret!

'What the devil does that mean, Master?'

'It's the name of a particular hexagram in the *Book of Changes*. When used as a sign in the practice of fortune telling, it means that people in high positions with soaring ambitions could suffer a turn of luck and have something to regret.'

'Something to regret. Hold on – is it meant as a warning for you?'

Without waiting for an answer, Yang picked up the knife again and examined it closely under the candlelight. It was extremely sharp. He placed a hair across the knife edge, which instantly cut the hair in two.

'This small knife is a precious one. Look at its hilt inlaid with no less than seven gemstones. It must have cost a small fortune,' Yang muttered. 'It could not have been thrown into your room as a practical joke.'

'No, but I don't think the note is necessarily meant for me. I'm far from having a high position at the present moment. As the saying goes, I'm more like a homeless dog running around looking for shelter.'

'You don't have to say that, Master. The new post may not appear to be as high as before, but the empress trusts you more than anybody else under the sun. Her Majesty may simply want you to enjoy a much-needed break and travel around for a short while, before some more important work is assigned to you.'

'Come on, Yang. For a man of my age, I want nothing more than a book with a cup of hot tea at home for a peaceful night. But you don't have to worry about the note. Go back to your room, Yang. It's past midnight.'

Instead, Yang scooped up a blanket draped over the arm of the other chair, wrapped himself in it, staring at the knife note, and kept on shaking his head like a rattle drum.

'No, the knife thrower – whoever or whatever he might be – did not want you to have a quiet night here. It must have come as a dire message for you, Master.'

As always, Yang was worrying – probably too much – for his master. Yang had been like that from the day he became Judge Dee's attendant/assistant and self-styled bodyguard.

Judge Dee was no less disturbed by the knife message; however, he tried to dispel Yang's uneasiness.

'We left just this morning. I decided to stay at this hostel on the spur of the moment, and we did not even register under our real names. How could the knife thrower possibly have known our whereabouts for the night? Perhaps it's simply a case of mistaken identity.'

Judge Dee chose not to discuss with Yang the possibility that they had been followed from their residence in the center of the capital all the way to the shabby hostel on its outskirts. He failed to figure out why people would have shadowed him like that and then thrown the ominous knife note. It did not add up. Still, he could not rule out the possibility.

'But it's a knife thrown with such accuracy – straight to the pillar beside you. And such a gem-decked knife, too. It's definitely a job done by a pro,' Yang said stubbornly. 'How could he have been wrong about the recipient of the message?'

'As I've mentioned, such a message is commonly given in terms of divination. As an ancient classic, the *Book of Changes* is a philosophical book of profound depth in its miraculous exploration of changes in the universal yin/yang system, but I do not believe in its application for fortune telling. So why bother?'

'How does that work for divination, Master?'

'I don't have the proper tools with me for a demonstration, but I can humor you with the help of copper coins,' he said, taking several coins out of his pocket. 'Heads and tails, you know. The result of your throws – in other words, the combination of heads and tails – make up the lines for yin and yang in a hexagram, and then you may consult the book for the meaning of that particular hexagram.'

'Please enlighten me, Master. I'm intrigued.'

Judge Dee threw the coins a couple of times, recorded the number of heads and tails in sequence, and then turned to take out the *Book of Changes* for its meaning.

'What?'

'Well, quite a surprise. *A hidden dragon should be careful in its movement*.'

'And its meaning?'

'At this stage, it's too early for the dragon to move about, so it won't hurt to stay put.'

'Another dragon! Too many mysterious coincidences for one night, Master,' Yang said, looking ghastly pale.

'Come on, you're worrying yourself sick for nothing, Yang. There's also a dragon in your nickname, isn't there? Go back to sleep in your room. It's late. And I'm getting really sleepy.'

Yang rose slowly with reluctance. He opened his mouth without managing to say anything. There was no disobeying his master.

As luck would have it, however, a loud, insistent knock on the door abruptly broke through the stillness of the night.

As Yang moved to open the door, Judge Dee hurried to put the knife and the note underneath a folder.

A middle-aged man in a gray cotton robe stood in the doorway, carrying a large envelope in his hand. He turned out to be a special messenger from Internal Minister Wu, Empress Wu's nephew, also the most powerful member of the Wu faction.

'Your Excellency' – the messenger knelt down in front of Judge Dee – 'Minister Wu knows that you are leaving the capital. He really admires your extraordinary talent as a judge, as you know, so he wants me to bring this special case report over to you tonight – the case report he has just received this afternoon of the sensational murder committed by Xuanji about ten days ago.'

'The sensational murder committed by the well-known poetess Xuanji?'

Judge Dee was more than surprised. It appeared to be somewhat unconventional for a powerful man like Minister Wu to consult about a murder case with a newly appointed circuit supervisor who was leaving the capital. A considerable number of officials under the powerful minister could have easily looked into the investigation of the case for him.

Not to mention the fact that Minister Wu had long considered Judge Dee as one of his arch-opponents at the court. His recent memorial to the empress was commonly seen as a deliberate effort to thwart the minister's attempt to change the dynasty of the Li family to that of the Wu family. They both knew this only too well. In fact, Dee's latest appointment was suspected by many to have been a result of the conspiracy pushed by Minister Wu. It was a well-calculated removal of the obstacle in his path to the supreme power of the Tang Empire.

'Her Majesty wants me to take over the new post as soon as possible, so I set out early this morning,' Dee said slowly without pulling out the case report. 'I'm sorry, I'm afraid I cannot afford to tarry around here.'

'The minister says that the case is becoming such a sensational one, involving not only a celebrated poetess, but a number of well-known men of letters, too. And people are talking about it as a case symbolic of the moral decline in today's empire. Your help will be crucial in ensuring a quick conclusion of the case in the interest of maintaining political stability for the Empire. You may need to spend just a couple of days taking a quick look into the case. It won't interfere at all with your reporting to the new post on time.'

So saying, the messenger remained kneeling on the ground. Apparently, Minister Wu had been well informed of Judge Dee's whereabouts, and of the deadline for him to report to his new official post, too.

'Minister Wu may have a point, I think. It is a sensational case indeed. So I'll spend a couple of days more here, but no longer, and not as a judge – I have to make that clear. I'll see what I can do as a sort of a private consultant, and I'll keep your master informed.'

'Thank you so much, Your Excellency.'

Much relieved, the messenger kowtowed, rose, and left like the wind.

'Who is Xuanji?' Yang asked the moment the messenger vanished out of sight.

'I've heard something about the Xuanji case. She is a young, beautiful, and talented poetess and courtesan – in her early or mid-twenties. If I'm interested at all in her case, to tell the truth, it's because I've read a lot of poems written by her. Much better than my own, that I have to admit, but with so much political trouble on my hands of late, I have not paid any serious attention to the murder case.'

'What kind of a murder case, Master?'

'About ten days ago, on the third day of the month, as a well-known poetess and a much-sought-after courtesan, Xuanji was entertaining several guests at a lunch party in the Xianyi Nunnery—'

'A poetess/courtesan entertaining her guests at a lunch party in the nunnery? It's absurd.'

'That's something intriguing in itself. The nunnery was where she stayed, but she's there not exactly as a Daoist nun. How she ended up being in a nunnery – I would have to do more research about that. Anyway, after lunch, one of her guests walked out into the backyard, where he was struck by a weird scene – a bevy of blue-headed flies buzzing, circling around a spot in a corner of the backyard. Nothing suspicious appeared on the surface. He waved at the flies, which flew away but immediately came buzzing back. He tried several times without success before he leaned down and noticed that the soil around the spot looked newly loosened.

'Then Xuanji hurried over to his side, sweating profusely, her face bleached of color. It was not a warm day, but she kept on wiping sweat from her forehead.

'The guest did not say anything about her strange reaction, but after he left the nunnery, he lost no time reporting it to his cousin, an assistant in the mayor's office, who then came over to the nunnery in the late afternoon with a search warrant issued by Mayor Pei.

'So they started digging in the corner of the nunnery backyard. To their consternation, it was the body of Xuanji's maidservant, Ning, buried under the surface soil there. They removed the white cloth that had been wrapped around her welt-and-bruise-covered body, which was not decaying yet in spite of the weather, so the maidservant must have been buried just the day before.

'Xuanji failed to give any explanation for it. According to her, Ning had told her the day before about going to visit her family for two or three days, so Xuanji went out shopping by herself that morning. Apparently, Ning had not left as she had told Xuanji. Instead, she stayed on and was beaten to death in the nunnery and buried in the corner of the backyard.

'Consequently, Xuanji was taken into custody, but in spite of the brutal bludgeoning at the courtroom, she insisted she did not know anything about Ning's death. A couple of days later, however, she suddenly confessed in prison, saying that on the second day of the month, she had gotten so drunk that she started beating Ning for some provocation she could not remember, kicking and whipping her violently until the latter passed out, and then she herself passed out, too. Once she was sober again, she saw there was no sign of life in the maidservant lying cold on the floor.

'Panic-stricken, Xuanji dragged the body out into the backyard and buried her under the cover of night. She thought that no one would notice a missing maid like Ning, and then she could make up a story of the maid quitting her service, and no one would have suspected any foul play in the nunnery. Little did she think that the flies circling above the corner of the backyard would give her away the very next day.'

'The body was not properly buried – not deep enough. A courtesan might not have had enough strength to do a good job of digging deep enough for the burial,' Yang said, nodding. 'Those blue-headed flies must have smelled the blood oozing underneath the surface soil.'

'In her statement made in prison, she provided some new details about the burial, saying she had a hard time finding the right tool for it, and that she was too frail a woman to have done the job properly in the dark of night.'

'That makes sense,' Yang said, 'but why has the murder case not yet been concluded even though she made the confession in prison?'

'I don't really know,' Judge Dee said, shaking his head. 'Perhaps the confession does not sound so convincing. And the mayor needs to look further into it. Anyway, a very strange case indeed.'

'But there must be something else in the case. For a special messenger to come overnight to you from Minister Wu, it's more than strange. It's like the old proverb about a skunk sneaking over to say "Happy New Year" to a rooster. It was definitely not done with good intentions. We cannot be too careful, Master.'

'Don't worry too much about it, Yang. It's not our case, nor am I intrigued by it.'

That was not exactly true, though. Judge Dee *was* intrigued. For a murder case involving the number-one poetess of the Tang Empire, it actually presented a personal challenge to him as well.

Not to mention the knife note and the message from Minister Wu.

Outside, the night watchman was making another round, beating the wooden knocker in a monotonous pattern against the night as it retreated further into the darkness.

Judge Dee knew he would have to do such a lot of work before he could get anywhere in the investigation, for which he had neither the time nor the authority.

'What are you thinking about, Master?'

'No, it does not have to be our case. And it is not our case. Now you go back to sleep in your room. I, too, have to doze for a little while if I want to get up in a decent condition in the morning.'

'It soon will be morning anyway, Master.'

After Yang went back to his room, Dee lit another candle, sat up straight with his back stiff like a bamboo stick, and took out the case report along with a new authorization note signed by Minister Wu earlier in the day.

It is stated that the bearer of this document hereby has the full authorization of the Internal Ministry to investigate the Xuanji case.

But Judge Dee did not think he had promised the minister anything. It would have been a different story if it had been an imperial order from the empress. As it was, in spite of Wu's assurance and the authorization note, Judge Dee could not help seeing something suspicious in the request.

He started reading the case report in earnest. For the moment, sleep was the furthest thing from his mind. Rubbing his eyes, he glimpsed a moth-like insect whirling around like crazy, circling and circling the candle flame.

The case report hardly offered anything new, however, to add to what Judge Dee had already learned from other sources.

He had read quite a number of Xuanji's poems, so he thought he might have a better understanding of the complicated poetess than the author of the case report.

Still, it was a puzzling case. The lack of a convincing motive on her part was something much discussed by people. But that was probably only one of the main reasons why the murder case remained unclosed.

In the case report, some of her neighbors actually attributed the murder to the evil influence of a bewitching black fox spirit that haunted the neighborhood of the nunnery, and in a paradoxical variation of that theory, she was the black fox spirit incarnate, revealing her true nature when she was dead drunk.

How such a superstitious assumption could have been woven into the official case report puzzled him.

A cricket started chirping eerily outside the window, from the backyard of the hostel – or from the very beginning of a poem by Xuanji.

The crickets chirruping in confusion
by the stone steps, the crystal-clear
dewdrops glistening on the tree leaves
in the mist-enveloped courtyard . . .

That was a poem composed for one of her lovers named Wen Tingyun, also one of the most prominent poets of the contemporary Tang Empire, but Judge Dee was unable to recall the title of the poem or the lines that followed.

He had read her work piece by piece, but in a far from systematic way. It took time and money to have a poetry collection published these days, and it was almost out of the question for a poetess to do so, he supposed, in the days when the Confucianist orthodoxy claimed that a woman's virtue comes in the absence of any intellectual talent.

It was then that an idea came flashing through his mind. There was something for him to do, it dawned on him. Something meaningful in itself.

He would have a collection of her poems compiled, and in the course of the compilation, he would be able to learn a bit more about her life.

For all he knew, what he had been achieving in the official world would eventually sink into oblivion. But Xuanji's poems would not. Judge Dee had reached an age when he could admit to himself what he was capable of doing or not. For one thing, he knew he would not be able to write such exquisite lines as hers, so the compilation of a volume for the beautiful, ill-fated poetess would probably be a project worth attempting in itself.

What's more, it would serve at the same time as a plausible cover for the investigation – or for the non-existent investigation. At least it could prove to be something for him to give Minister Wu to show that he had tried.

A sparkle sputtered from the candle that was burning out in the hostel room. He could not help nodding to the reflection of the old, bookish man in the bronze mirror, which he usually used to adjust his official black cap.

It brought about another inexplicable wave of weariness that overwhelmed him.

The next morning, he might be able to think a bit more clearly, he reflected, nodding again.

Finally, he began to doze off, still sitting stiff like a bamboo stick in the hard wooden chair. The first gray of the morning appeared to be peeping in through the paper window like a soft-footed fox.

Heavy-eyed, Dee became aware of another man entering the room, heading straight to the seat opposite, across the table from him, the knife still trembling in the pillar overhead between them.

The newcomer turned out to be another candidate at the capital civil service examination, a close friend whose surname was Qiao, in his early twenties, who began talking with Dee in high spirits. Confident of their success with flying colors in the capital examination, they were trying to compose poems about what they were going to do for the Great Tang Empire.

Young men's aspiration should be catching the cloud in the high skies . . .

In the skies, all of a sudden, they saw their years flying away like a forsaken kite with its string snapped . . . Now, both of them with their hair streaked with white, they begin debating heatedly in retrospect.

'But what have you really become, Judge Dee?'

'A fat, old, obsequious survivor in the system, I admit. But give the devil her due, Her Majesty is a capable empress, and the contemporary Tang Empire under her rule is enjoying a better, more prosperous time than ever before.'

'How could a nun-turned-imperial-concubine have justifiably turned into the supreme ruler on the throne in light of the orthodox Confucianism? Alas, you have studied all the classics for nothing!'

'But one has to do things within the system, Qiao. The empress is a wise benevolent dictator, so to speak, and capable of listening to the good, capable people who care about the welfare of the country.'

'But aren't you ashamed of standing side by side with those people capable only of pleasing her in bed?'

'What's the point of dwelling so much on her private life? After all, she never mixes the private with the public.'

'The empress knows you are loyal to her, but at the same time, to the Li family as well. The double allegiance is not something she would easily forget or forgive, Judge Dee. You'd better brace yourself for the consequences.'

'I understand, Qiao.'

'You don't understand. Be aware of the signs of dragons you have just seen, Judge Dee—'

Another knife came flying in, aiming not at the pillar, but at the dragon soaring in the snow, stretching across a long scroll of classical Chinese painting on the wall . . .

TWO

Judge Dee woke with a start. The scenes from his dream began fading fast like ignorant armies shouting, clashing in confused alarms of fighting in the fast-retreating night. Rubbing his eyes, disoriented, he found his blue cotton gown drenched in cold sweat.

The candle had burned itself out on the table, with white wax drops scattered around the stub, and a faint smell still lingering in the air.

The bare, crumbling wall presented no painting of a dragon soaring across the swirling snow, nor was there any visitor from his younger days sitting opposite at the table. The light of the early morning began streaming into the hostel room.

Dee did not believe in the interpretation of dreams. But the reappearance of the dragon signs in association with the earlier ones from the *Book of Changes* filled his heart with an uncanny trepidation.

He started to contemplate the feasibility of finding a different approach to the murder case, though he kept reminding himself that he'd better investigate under the cover of something else.

Pulling away the sweat-soaked blue robe, he put on a black one with a subdued pattern, adjusting his cap again in the bleary reflection of the bronze mirror. It represented an apparition of the figure both strange and familiar, totally unlike the one in that nearly forgotten dream.

He was trying to recapture some details in the dream scene, taking a small sip at the cold tea, when he heard a light knock on the door.

Turning over his shoulder, he saw Yang pushing the door open soundlessly, carrying a wooden breakfast tray, and frowning at the sight of the unslept-in bed, before his glance swept around to Judge Dee who was still sitting stiffly at the table.

Yang, too, might not have slept a wink after their discussion about the knife message.

'Nothing really tasty from the small hostel kitchen, Master,' Yang said, placing the tray on the table. 'So I've bought for you an earthen oven cake and salty soybean soup from a street-corner vendor.'

'Well, a cup of Dragon Well tea would be perfect for the moment, preferably fresh and hot from a cotton-padded teapot warmer.'

It would be too much of a luxury to have hot water all the time at the shabby hostel, Judge Dee knew.

'But you have to eat something, Master. Especially after such a long night. The steaming soybean soup strewn with chopped green onion and purple seaweed tastes quite delicious. Then it'll be high time for you to leave Chang'an. It's a long trip ahead of you today.'

Apparently, Yang saw no point their staying any longer in the capital. It appeared to be a legitimate move for Judge Dee to set off despite the request made by Minister Wu. After all, Judge Dee had the imperial decree issued directly from the empress for him to go to the new post.

'Yes, let's move,' Judge Dee said reflectively, rubbing his temple with a finger, 'but to a temple in the Fang Mountains first. Dingguo Temple.'

'What!'

'It's a small temple, but well known for its fabulous vegetarian meals. A lot of gourmet tourists go to the Buddhist temple for that reason. It's on the way. So we shall make a visit there first.'

'Very well, then, we'll stop for lunch there. Have something light and nutritious,' Yang said with a suggestion of relief in his voice. 'That's exactly what you need.'

'And we may as well stay at the temple for a day or two. I'm thinking of arranging a Buddhist service in the temple for my late parents. I don't know when I can possibly make it back to the capital, you know.' Judge Dee added after a short pause, 'It's quite close to Xuanji's nunnery, just about a mile or two away. You and I can also take a look there.'

'But we don't have to do anything for the case, as you said last night – surely not for the sake of Minister Wu.'

'Well, it does not hurt to make a show of doing something

about it as requested by Minister Wu. We don't really have to go out of the way for it. In fact, there's something else I would like to do, Yang.'

'What's that?'

'I've read a number of her touching poems, and heard a lot of anecdotes about her colorful life. A very intriguing character, that celebrated poetess named Xuanji. So I'm toying with the idea of compiling a poetry collection for her. A temple will be quiet and convenient for that purpose. After the knife message last night, staying in this hostel is no longer a good idea.'

'Whatever you say, then, Master.'

A short while later, stepping out of the hostel, Yang abruptly turned and said, his eyes squinting in the sunlight, 'I don't think it's a good idea to go to the temple, Master. The temple is still very much on the outskirts of the capital.'

'You are worrying too much,' Judge Dee said, stepping up into the carriage prepared for him.

It was out of the question for him to conduct the investigation openly, but a short stay at the temple for a Buddhist service as well as for the compilation of a poetry collection would sound like a plausible excuse for the judge, who was known among his colleagues for his passion for poetry, though hardly known as a poet compared with Xuanji.

As an integrated part of the civil service examination, poetry-writing in the Tang Empire was more than a fashion among men of letters. Success in the examination spelled a promising official career for the candidates. Successful or not in the examination, however, excellent poems alone could also bring the poets a sort of recognizable social status, and made their names remembered for 'thousands of autumns.' For those less talented writers of poetry, the compilation of a poetry collection would therefore make a considerable alternative.

'What's up . . .' Yang did not finish the question – perhaps with the words 'your sleeve?' He had encountered unexpected changes of plan on Judge Dee's part numerous times. 'Whatever you decide to do, you don't have to stay at a temple for that, Master. It's not difficult to find a better hostel nearby.'

'Like hostels, Dingguo Temple provides room and board for its visitors. For men of letters, a stay in the temple is also considered far more desirable, and fashionable, too. You may not know that well-known poets like Meng Haoran or Wang Zhihuan wrote poems on the temple walls, and then people came to the temple for the purpose of reading and copying the poems.'

'Yes, you may well write a couple of poems on the temple wall, too, Master.'

'No, I know better. I've not written a good line for years. My poems on the temple wall would be a joke for thousands of years. But I've heard that a poet monk named Han Shan happens to be staying there at the moment. A real celebrity in the circle of poets, he should be able to tell me something more about the poetess. The biographical details could be valuable for the collection, you know.'

'But you don't have to compile a poetry collection of hers at this critical juncture, Master.'

'Well, a man has to try his hand at the impossible mission.'

'You have quoted this Confucianist epigram so many times. Possible or impossible, as long as it's the right mission for you to accomplish.'

'You know me, Yang.'

'It is fine if you insist,' Yang said with a touch of resignation, 'but I will have to stay with you all the time in the temple.'

'You're being overprotective again, Yang, but I'll have two rooms booked, no problem.'

'To the temple, then! Sit tight, Master.'

The carriage started rolling slowly along the trail. It was quite bumpy and slippery after the off-and-on drizzle throughout the night. Driving the carriage in front, Yang made occasional comments in between the whip cracking through the stillness of the surrounding hills.

'You may well take a break in the carriage, Master, after the disturbance of last night's knife note. I really don't like it.'

Yang was not overreacting to the knife note left at the hostel the previous night, Dee reflected, still far from sleepy, even though he had slept little during the night. With the unexpected request from Minister Wu, the message in the knife note seemed to have become even more inexplicably sinister.

In accordance with the message reinforced with the *Book of Changes*, Judge Dee had better stay put. It was perhaps a coincidence that the second reading in the light of the coin consultation with the Confucian classic carried a similar implication. A deep-dyed Confucian scholar, Dee could not help taking the message seriously. Any drastic movement on his part could lead to disastrous consequences.

Didn't the authorization letter from Minister Wu mean, however, that Judge Dee had to move on?

But he could not but remind himself again that the message in the knife note spelled an opposite direction that he should follow.

Another cracking of the whip in front, Yang could be heard heaving a dramatic sigh, characteristic of the overprotective assistant as before – as always.

Time flies. It was more than a dozen years since Judge Dee had seen Yang for the first time. At the time, Yang was rotting in prison for beating up a young rogue from an official family who attacked a poor girl in a wet market. Judge Dee managed to snatch Yang out of prison and clear his name from the false accusation. There and then, Yang declared kneeling at Judge Dee's foot in the dust, 'Master, you've given me a second life, and from now on it belongs to you alone.'

Yang had kept his words all these years, proving to be a more valuable assistant than expected – skilled in Shaolin martial arts, street-smart, incessantly energetic – and, more than anything else, intensely loyal to Judge Dee, guarding him all the way through the ups and downs in his official career.

Time changes a lot.

Some people changed; however, some people did not.

But how could a celebrated, talented poetess like Xuanji have turned into a diabolical murderer in such a shorter period of time?

The deep yearning in those sentimental poems of hers might have not changed, though.

The music floating from the neighbors
under the moonlight, I look out, alone,
from the high tower to the far-away view
of the lambent mountains. The wind chilly
on the bamboo mattress, I can only express
my sadness through the decorated zither . . .

Were those lines she wrote in that poem to Wen? Or were they in another poem? Or to someone else? Judge Dee was confused again. Nor was he sure about its being the entire poem or not. As far as he could recollect, the poem seemed to end in a more explicit complaint about her inconsolable solitude.

Frustrated with the elusive memory, Judge Dee concluded he was getting old.

'See, there's a yellowish banner behind the turn of the mountain trail,' Yang said, breaking into Judge Dee's somber reveries. 'That's it, the temple banner, I think. The temple is not located far from the hostel.'

The carriage was already slowing down.

At the entrance to the temple, Judge Dee was greeted by a receptionist monk named Nameless. Possibly in his mid-twenties, with a round face and alert eyes, Nameless bowed respectfully in a red, ample-sleeved silk cassock.

'I've heard that the well-known poet monk Han Shan is staying at your temple, right?' Judge Dee lost no time in raising the question.

'Yes, Han Shan has been here for a month, and possibly for half a month more.'

'That's fantastic. I would like to have two rooms booked next to his. One for me, one for my assistant. We'll stay for a couple of days at least. It's a great opportunity for me to meet and talk with Han Shan here.'

'But Han Shan does not talk to everyone, as you may know,' Nameless said with a suggestion of hesitance, scratching his shaved bald head. 'And there may not be any vacant rooms at the moment.'

Judge Dee gave him a handwritten name card and then added a small piece of silver. 'Please give my card to the poet monk. He knows me. And here is something small for your trouble in making the room arrangement for us. It's a celebrated temple with a lot of visitors, I know.'

Nameless cast a look at the name card and nodded with astonishment written on his face before he accepted the silver, stuffing it into the ample sleeve.

'Confucius says, "You cannot decline something from a senior gentleman." No trouble at all, Your Honor. I'll double-check the rooms.'

As Nameless hurried back into the temple to check the availability of rooms, Yang moved up to his master in strides.

'For this morning,' Judge Dee said, 'you don't have to stay here with me. I'll probably have a long talk with Han Shan about poetry. But there's one thing you can do for me. Go and find a copy of Xuanji's poetry collection.'

'That will not be a problem. I'll go up to the town, and there I may also be able to take a walk around her neighborhood. But you really must be careful, Master. The temple is not far from the hostel.'

'Don't worry about me, Yang, and you take care of yourself, too.'

With Yang's figure retreating out of sight into the mountain trail, Han Shan came out in hurried steps, bowing to Dee from a distance. A tall man with a square ruddy face, dreamy eyes, and a clean-shaven head, Han Shan was wearing a blue cassock in tatters and threadbare straw sandals, more like a humble servant to Nameless who was walking behind.

Having probably learned something more about Judge Dee's official status inside the temple, Nameless was now all smiles, saying in an obsequious voice, 'Our humble place is so brightened by your visit, Your Honor. One of the two rooms is ready, and the other one will soon be ready for you, too.'

'No hurry. I'll have a talk with my old friend Han Shan first. And my assistant Yang is running an errand for me in the neighborhood. When he comes back, you may take him directly to his room.'

Rubbing his eyes with a yawn, Han Shan began reciting like an actor stepping on to the lit stage:

'Generals in iron armors surmounting
the mountain passes at night,
ministers waiting in the cold
for the early-morning Court session,
a monk still lying on bed with the sun
shining high over the temple –
fame and gain are nothing
when compared with leisure.'

'What a delightful poem, Han Shan!'

'Alas, it's not mine. Nameless has just woken me up for the visit of a high-ranking official like you.'

'Come on, I'm no high-ranking official – not any longer. If only I could afford to enjoy leisure like you, totally worry-free in a mundane world full of worries!' Judge Dee said, aware of a satirical reminder Han Shan was making of the difference between the two of them.

'Well, leisure is available only for a useless man like me. But it's a long time no see, Judge Dee. At least three or four years since we last met in Suzhou.'

'In Suzhou, the temple nowadays is so well known because of you – Han Shan Temple.'

'No, it's well known because of the cold mountains there in the winter. That's what the temple name "*Han Shan*" really means. I'm just lucky enough to find a shelter in it.'

And then it was Judge Dee's turn to start reciting.

'The moon setting, the crow cawing,
the frost spreading out against the sky,
the maple tree standing out on the bank,
the fisherman's light moving
across the river, who is there,
full of worries even in sleep?

By the Han Shan Temple,
out of Gusu City,
a sampan comes
in the midnight bells.'

'So you have memorized that poem by Zhang Ji, that's wonderful, Judge Dee, but "Mooring by the Maple Bridge at Night" is a poem written about the temple, not about me.'

'But you are the temple, and the temple is you, right? That's exactly what a Zen master has said about enlightenment, and what you have said in a poem of yours, I think, but such an insightful understanding is unobtainable to an ignorant layman like me, Han Shan.'

'Come on, you haven't come to discuss Zen poetry with me here, Judge Dee.'

'To say the least, Zhang Ji's is a poem inspired and influenced by you, Han Shan. You don't have to be that modest to me.'

With the poems and pleasantries exchanged between the two, they were ushered into a room, barely furnished except for the black wood shelves lined up with books and scriptures, and a dark wood table with four chairs around. It looked more like a meditation enclave for the senior monks. A shaft of sunlight languidly penetrated through the lattice paper window into the room.

A small monk came in and placed on the table two cups and a teapot wrapped in a cotton-padded cover, and a wooden bowl that contained shelled pine nuts.

'I've just learned that you're staying in the temple,' Judge Dee said, dropping a white pine nut into his mouth, 'so before leaving the capital for a new post, I want to spend two or three days, for a change, just in leisure and peace like you.'

'No, you have your karma-informed path, and I, mine. In this mundane world of ours, things as insubstantial as a drop of water, or a peck by a bird, all are predestined and predestining. You're bound to do great things as a capable official in the Tang Empire, Judge Dee. There's nothing for me to do as a monk, however, except chanting scripture and writing a line or two in a secluded temple.' Han Shan smiled a knowing smile before going on, 'As in an old proverb, people do not come to the temple without having to pray to the Buddhist image for some special favor. So go ahead and tell me what you want.'

'Indeed, there's such a lot to catch up for old friends like you two,' said Nameless, smiling with a knowing nod. He rose and excused himself readily from the room.

As the two of them were left alone in the room, Judge Dee took a small sip at the tea and resumed, 'Well, among other things, I'm trying to compile a collection of poems by Xuanji. Maybe you can give me some suggestions for the project. And that's the favor I'm asking of you here in the temple.'

'Is it a project worth pursuing for our celebrated Judge Dee?' Han Shan looked up from the cup, a wry smile spreading across his face, deepening the lines on his forehead. 'Of course you write poems, too, as everyone knows.'

'It's not about my poems, you know. Her poems have been circulating only in a limited circle. If nothing is done about it right now, a number of them may soon get lost.'

'You mean after her execution?'

'It's a possibility, isn't it? I'm not the judge for the case at the present moment, but I may say that it's the most likely conclusion. As an admirer of her poems, such a project is the order of the day. Questions about those poems, textual or contextual, would better be answered while she's still available.'

'That's true. But as a poet yourself, why don't you try to compile a collection of Judge Dee's poems?'

'I've been so busy with official responsibilities. I did not come to really appreciate her works until the breakout of the murder case. So I have read or reread a number of her poems of late. It's true I've written some myself, but compared with hers, not a single line of mine will be passed down to readers in the future, and I'm sure about that.'

'Well, I remember one poem of yours, which is about the empress offering the sacrifice to Heaven on top of the Tai Mountains. That poem will be read for generations and generations, I bet.'

'Come on. You're making fun of me. It's nothing but an aggregation of pompous words required for that occasion. If it's read by people at all, it's not because of the merit of the poem, but because of Her Majesty on that historical occasion.'

'But that sounds just like a piece composed by the loyal,

talented Judge Dee whom the empress really trusts. So much for poetry,' Han Shan said with another knowing smile. 'What do you want me to do for you today?'

'Tell me what you know about Xuanji's life and work. As well-known poets, you two must have frequently met and mixed with each other in the circle. These biographical details will be helpful, especially for a "confessional poet" like her. A considerable number of her poems were written for her lovers and "close friends" – full of the details of their intimacies.'

'I've met her several times, mostly at social parties, and for an absurd reason you may have never thought of, Judge Dee. With her, a beautiful, fashionable poet courtesan, and me, a crazy, impoverished poet monk, we were put together just like two exotic side dishes added to a grand banquet. It makes sense, needless to say, from a gourmet perspective.'

'Exactly, perspectives make meanings.'

'She's a gifted poet, no question about it. But what makes her poetry a success is – at least partially – because of the sad, salacious, sentimental stories about her with those heartless lovers behind these poems.'

'You're right, Han Shan. You know what? With my so-called successful official career, I've had no time for poems – nor for any authentic or soul-touching experience, from which wonderful poems originate. And that's the very reason for my mediocre writing, I have to say.'

'Spare me your self-pity, Judge Dee. It's extravagant of you to indulge in it. But you're a busy official, that much I do know. Without further ado, let me start telling you what I know about her.'

'Yes, please go ahead, Han Shan, with all the details you can think of.'

Instead of immediately launching into a detailed narrative, Han Shan tapped on the table with two fingers, frowned in the ensuing silence, and put down his teacup on the saucer with a surprising clink.

Outside the window, a large green leaf fell swirling down to the courtyard.

* * *

'Xuanji was born into a poor family,' Han Shan began narrating in the quiet temple room, coughing to clear his throat. 'When only five or six, she showed an exceptional passion for poetry, which, unfortunately, turned into too much of a luxury for her family. For her brush pens and ink, for instance, her mother had to do extra loads of laundry for the neighbors at night. While still a teenager, she started writing poems in earnest. According to those who read them at the time, her works appeared to be extraordinarily mature and accomplished for her age. Soon her name spread far and wide. It attracted poets and scholars, like schools of silver carp rushing downstream, who could not help feeling drawn toward such a young talented beautiful poetess.

'And then Wen Tingyun, one of the top poets of our time, also came to visit her. A long-time passionate fan of Wen, Xuanji was overwhelmed by his unexpected presence.

'Like others, Wen did not believe that a young girl like her could have penned those excellent lines. So he chose a topic – "Willow Trees by the River" – for her to compose the poem there and then in his presence. It was conventional, as you know, for a senior poet to give a young one such a test.

'She dashed off the poem right on the spot. What's even more surprising, in spite of the title, the word "willow" did not even appear once in the whole piece. At the same time, it's definitely a poem about a willow tree by the river. The contents and techniques of the poem spoke a lot about a young, gifted girl with soaring literary aspirations.'

'Yes, I've heard of it. A marvelous poem indeed,' Dee said nodding before he started reciting:

'The verdant trees stretching long
along the desolate bank, a tower distantly
dissolving into the faint mist,
petals falling, falling over an angler,
with the reflection rippling
on the autumn water,
the old tree's root turning
into a secluded fish-hiding spot,
and the twigs low-hanging,

tying a sampan –
I'm startled out of a dream:
the night of roaring wind and rain
is infused with my new worries.'

'Wow, you've memorized it, Judge Dee. Little wonder, given your passion for poetry. Her poem is extraordinary. And it came as no surprise that the poem moved Wen so much that he gave a rave review in front of other poets there. Quite a lot of people gathered around on that occasion. That instantly established her status as one of the top poetesses of the Tang Empire. Indeed, the poem is a must for that collection of yours. An extraordinary poem by any standard. It was then Wen's turn to be overwhelmed by her, as you may easily imagine. She was young, attractive, brilliant – and crazy about him, too.'

'Now I have a question for you, Han Shan. There's something between Wen and Xuanji. No one can miss it in those dewy-eyed poems she wrote for him. While he's much older, by thirty years or so, an affair between the two still seemed to be romantically irresistible to her. Apparently, she's more than ready to throw herself into his arms. Why did it not work out for the pair of them in the end?'

'There are numerous interesting interpretations about the inscrutable relationship between the two. As some people speculated, Wen was not sure whether Xuanji was pursuing him as a way to climb up the social ladder herself. According to others, Wen simply suffered a sort of inferiority complex because he was a very plain-looking man, particularly so in the company of the young, beautiful Xuanji.

'According to the most popular interpretation, however, Wen was too self-conscious of his social status because of his failure in the civil service examination. If he married a poor girl like Xuanji, his dream of moving up in society could come to an immediate end, so he balked in spite of all the poems she sent to him as well as those he sent to her. Family background can be of such great importance in our Tang Empire. Whatever the interpretation, though, they kept writing passionate poems for each other, which puzzles a lot of people.'

'What a pity! I would really love to put those poems together for a special section – she for Wen, and Wen for her – which would probably cover the best pieces she has written.'

'Alternatively, you may have a special collection of her love poems, including those written for others as well as for Wen, with a title such as "Love Poems between Xuanji and Her Men."'

'More than one man! Yes, that could be a truly tantalizing title for a best-selling poetry collection. Thanks for the suggestion, Han Shan.'

Such a suggestion from a poet monk was a surprise. In his younger days, Han Shan too might have had his share, however, of romantic illusions and disillusions in the world of red dust before he escaped into Buddhism.

'In fact, I first came to know Xuanji through Wen – through stories and gossip about the romance between the two,' Han Shan went on after taking another deliberate sip of the tea. 'It was paradoxical that a group of Wen's poems were written with a female persona complaining about her unreciprocated love, as if echoing from the bottom of her heart. And with her perspective, too. According to several critics, those poems of Wen's must have meant a great deal to her.'

'Yes, that's unusual, but not without precedent. In the classical Chu tradition, men of letters wrote love poems as a way of showing their loyalty to the supreme ruler – comparing themselves to neglected beauties pining away because of their cold-hearted lords.'

'Have you read the one titled "The Islet Enclosed in White Duckweed"? A love poem with a female persona informed by such helpless pining.' Han Shan breathed into the tea with a dramatic pause before he started to read:

'After applying her make-up,
she stands leaning against the balcony,
looking out to the river, alone,
to thousands of sails passing along –
none is the one she waits for.

The sun setting slant,
the water running silent, long,

her heart is breaking
at the sight of the islet enclosed
in white duckweed.'

'The speaker's voice is surely Xuanji's in that poem by Wen. You're so right about that, Han Shan.'

'They kept on writing for each other. She was the more explicit one, going so far as to call her poems, quite unashamedly, her love letters to Wen.

'Then Wen did something unbelievable. He introduced her to Zi'an, the number-one successful candidate in the capital civil service examination—'

'Wen actually put the two of them together as a matchmaker?'

'And for that matter, a materialistic matchmaker to boot. Zi'an was a far more worthy match than Wen in the eyes of the mundane world: younger, more wealthy, more handsome, and with a much more promising future, and he was waiting alone in Chang'an to be assigned an official post.'

'But why should a romantic poet like Wen have chosen to do that, Han Shan?'

'It's possible that Wen cared for her in his way, so he tried to secure for her a better future in the company of Zi'an instead. At least, so it might have appeared to Wen. As for her, whatever feelings she might have cherished for Wen, she knew better as a realistic girl. But there's a catch . . .'

'Alas, there's always a catch.'

'Zi'an was married to someone from the illustrious Pei family. Still, it was not uncommon for a well-to-do man to have a concubine or two. The first poem in the *Book of Songs*, for instance, describes the scene of a virtuous queen in ancient China picking up a young pretty girl and welcoming her home as a concubine for her lord.'

'Yes, a poem about the virtuous queen indeed,' Judge Dee exclaimed, taking a sip of the cold tea. 'In accordance with the critics of the Five Classics, the poem embodies the so-called queenly virtue.'

'For a woman of Xuanji's poor family background, to be a concubine to Zi'an appeared nonetheless an acceptable choice, so she moved in with him. For a short while, things seemed to be working out for the two of them; they were said to be "writing love poems on one another's bodies" in bed. However, happy days are always so short. His wife came to join him in the capital. There was no keeping it a secret from her anymore. Xuanji had imagined that they could manage to get along like other families, with the wife and the concubines living under the same roof – sometimes in the same bed. Xuanji was willing to play second fiddle in the family, but Zi'an's wife turned out to be an insanely jealous tigress. She made a point of making Xuanji's life miserable all the time, and it did not take long for her to finally drive Xuanji out.

'A hen-pecked husband, Zi'an was in no position to fight for Xuanji. His official career could have been compromised in the event of a divorce, with his wife from such a noble family. Instead, he donated a sum to a Daoist nunnery on the outskirts of Chang'an, so that Xuanji at least had a temporary place to stay – a place not too far away, so that he might be able to pay a short visit to her in secret.'

'Somewhat like me,' Judge Dee said, 'a place to stay in the Buddhist temple here. It's fashionable in a way – and close to a celebrated poet monk.'

'Enough, Judge Dee. For you, it's just for a day or two's leisure. But an indefinite time period for her.'

'That's true. And it's a shrewd move on Zi'an's part,' Judge Dee said, adding hot tea to Han Shan's cup. 'Going to the nunnery could signify a break from one's past. A new way of living, so to speak, though she did not have to behave like a nun. A nun in name, she's still able to receive visitors such as Wen or Zi'an. With the temple door closed at night, what they could have done would not be too difficult for anyone to imagine.

'Off the record, didn't the Empress Wu – long before she became the empress – enter a Daoist temple for a while as a Daoist nun as well? I bet it was out of the same consideration.'

Judge Dee knew what the poet monk was referring to. In her earlier days, Empress Wu had once served as a 'palace female talent' for the first emperor Li Shimin of the Tang

Empire, who was said to have taken a liking to her. What might have happened in the royal palace was not difficult to imagine. And it was conventional that after the emperor's death, those palace women who had been touched by the divine ruler would then have to stay single, huddled up for life in seclusion. However, the new emperor, Li Zhi, the son of the late emperor, actually fell head over heels for Wu. One thing leading to another, as a 'palace female talent' for the old emperor, Wu became an imperial concubine for the young emperor, a dramatic turn that appeared so scandalous, so intolerable to the orthodox Confucianist officials. When she was declared empress after the death of Li Zhi, she eventually found herself sitting on the throne as the supreme ruler of the whole nation. Of late, she had even tried to rename the Tang Empire as the Zhou Empire and to move the capital from Chang'an to Luoyang. Such a metamorphosis was naturally unacceptable to those who pledged allegiance to the Tang Dynasty of the Li family, and as a result, one rebellion after another broke out, but without any success.

Han Shan chose not to say too much as Judge Dee happened to be an orthodox Confucianist too, who protested against such moves on the part of the empress, yet, at the same time, was a senior trusted official serving under Empress Wu.

'From time to time, Zi'an was able to sneak into the temple,' Han Shan went on, changing the subject. 'Xuanji had hoped that he would manage to eventually get her out of the nunnery, as he had promised, but Zi'an was then assigned to an official post far away from the capital. It was a matter of course for him to travel to the new post with his wife, and Xuanji was left alone in the nunnery. She was devastated by what she considered as his callous betrayal.

'As the proverb says, it does not matter if you hurl a broken urn to the ground – it's already broken anyway. She abandoned herself to despair, and then to debauchery. It did not take her long to start seeing men there in the open, night after night. With the reputation of the nunnery irreparably damaged, the abbess fled in the night, and Xuanji took it over as her own domain. She had a colorful banner displayed outside declaring, "Poetry Talk with Xuanji," which provided a convenient pretext for her to receive men, and for the visitors to the nunnery as well. She turned into something of a high-class poetess/courtesan, cultivating connections for herself by hook or by crook, accepting money and gifts and favors and whatever else, though she did not necessarily have to pay it back with her body in bed, at least not every time—'

'Sorry to interrupt you two, but it's time for lunch.' The reappearance of Nameless in the room broke off Han Shan's narrative. 'Our abbot Stainless is not feeling so well today, but he insists on my providing a special vegetarian meal for our two distinguished guests today. And he would like to meet you in person when he is better tomorrow.'

'Yes, the vegetarian meal here is absolutely incredible,' Han Shan said, nodding. 'You cannot afford to miss it.'

Walking down along the winding hill trail, Yang knew he had to deal with an assignment totally foreign to him.

It was in Judge Dee's field, the hunt for Xuanji's poetry collection, but Judge Dee had to talk to the poet monk at the temple for the day. So it was a necessary division of labor for the two of them. There were just a couple of days for them to conduct the investigation, and Yang had to take over the job from his master.

As far as Yang knew, people sold and bought books mostly in temple market fairs, but he had no idea about the market fair dates. Only one time had he followed Judge Dee into something like a bookstore in the center of the capital city, and it was too far away for him to make it there and back in just half a day.

But he recalled having visited a medium-sized small town nearby, so he headed there.

It did not take him long to reach the town, but to his confusion, he failed to find a single bookstore there – at least not in the strict sense of the word. In fact, most of the stores he came across not only sold books but carried a lot of other stuff as well. On one or two half-empty shelves of the third store he stepped into stood nothing but textbooks of Confucian classics, including *Book of Rites*, *Book of Songs*, and *Book of Changes*, all of which were the furthest thing from his mind.

The second shelf he was examining in a corner turned out to be more like an old rare book section, sporting several handwritten copies on display under an impressive array of silk scrolls of calligraphies and paintings hanging down from the white walls.

According to the store owner, some local poets and writers put a few of their handwritten manuscripts on sale there, but usually just a couple of pages, nothing close to a complete or well-edited collection.

'A woodblock printing edition can be very expensive. For a poet's collection, it is usually just a small print run. Not enough to cover the cost. Something like a vanity print, you know.'

So it might not be such a bad business idea for Judge Dee to compile a collection of Xuanji's poems, Yang observed, if that was what Judge Dee indeed planned to do – perhaps not too small a print run after Xuanji's execution, given the possibility it might gain wider attention and become a bestseller. Still, he doubted that his bookish master would throw himself into such a business venture.

Shifting his glance to a long silk scroll hung on the wall with a high price tag, Yang inquired whether Xuanji too had scrolls of calligraphies or paintings for sale in the store, either by herself or from other celebrities given to her as gifts.

Sure enough, the owner produced a silk scroll in Xuanji's own handwriting – a poem composed for a girl in the neighborhood, but toward the bottom left-hand corner of the scroll, there was a line written in smaller characters: *Copied out for Wei Hua as well.* Yang was no judge of poetry, but the silk scroll was marked with a fairly low price. He wondered who Wei Hua was, given they were willing to sell it so cheap to the shop.

'Wei Hua, one of her good-for-nothing lovers,' the store owner said disparagingly in response to Yang's inquiry. 'Wei sold everything practically the moment he got it from her. What an impossible, insatiable leech!'

Yang made a mental note, which might turn out to be a clue worth exploring, although he had no idea who Wei really was, or, for that matter, how many lovers Xuanji might have had.

Still, he went on playing the role of a diligent assistant in the presence of a curiosity dealer, purchasing the silk scroll after pretending to bargain for a short while. He also asked about Wei's address, as Xuanji might have left some other valuable things for the antique business.

'You really have an eye for the potential,' the store owner said approvingly. 'The price of her writing or paintings could soon go through the roof.'

'You mean after she is beheaded at the conclusion of the case?'

'Yes, she's doomed. It's obvious.'

'Well, is there anything else you've heard or learned about her?'

'You mean the murder case?'

'Yes. It's unimaginable for a talented young woman like her – only in her mid-twenties. My master has told me something about her.'

'I will ask around for you if you plan to come back. I may learn something about the poetess. Possibly get some more writing from her, too.'

'Of course I will come back here. Now, another curious question: in addition to those visitors or lovers to the nunnery, what kind of people did she mix with?'

'The nunnery is close to a village called Jiangling, so most of her neighbors there are ordinary villagers. She was not interested in mixing with them. Nor they with her – with one or two exceptions. One is a stationery dealer named Xiahou living in the village, with a small shop in town. He supplied her with things like paper, ink sticks, and brush pens. He once told me about her favorite fox-tail brush pen, which is obscenely expensive, as it is made of the hair from a rare scarlet fox tail.'

'Fox tail?'

'I'm not that sure about it – usually, it's made of skunk tail, the best-quality hair for a brush pen, but she's called a black fox spirit. Some people say she's literally a fox spirit, you know, even using a fox-tail brush pen. Who can really tell? You can talk to Xiahou about it. Another one close to Xuanji is a young flower girl at the southern end of the village. She sent her fresh flowers from time to time, for all those wild dinner parties in the nunnery.'

'Thanks. I'll definitely come back to you,' Yang said, thinking it was lunchtime and wondering what 'celebrated vegetarian meal' Judge Dee might be having with the poet monk in the temple.

The vegetarian meal in the temple was very fancy. Instead of serving it in the temple dining hall, the lunch was delivered into the room in which Judge Dee and Han Shan had been talking about Xuanji and the murder case. Nameless had the small monks carrying into the room a couple of two-tiered, red-painted bamboo baskets. It was considerate of Nameless to make sure that Judge Dee and Han Shan could continue talking in privacy.

In the midst of producing the steaming hot dishes out of the bamboo baskets and placing them on to the table, Nameless kept himself busy introducing each of the delicacies to Judge Dee and Han Shan with unmistakable pride in his voice.

'For today's lunch, we have extraordinary red braised pork, super fried rice paddy eels, exceptional bear prawns in white sauce, unbelievable spicy and tender beef tendon—'

'What a paradox,' Judge Dee commented. 'For a vegetarian meal, the dishes here appear to be all named in connection to meat and fish – non-vegetable.'

'For the people who can hardly keep the pot boiling, it's a matter of course for them to take meat and fish as the more desirable delicacies,' Han Shan said, 'so the names of meat and fish lend themselves to the delicious imagination. For most of the patrons of the temple, the vegetarian dishes here serve for a pleasant change, and those names simply make a vegetarian banquet more impressive, and more imaginative, too.'

'What is the "super fried rice paddy eel," then?'

'Extra-dry tofu sliced and fried like the real paddy eels, prepared with the same sauce,' Nameless explained, gesturing with his hand in imitation of cutting, deboning, and slicing the live rice paddy eel in the kitchen, 'topped with sizzling sesame oil on chopped green onion and golden ginger when the dish is served on the table.'

'Indeed, what's in a name?' Han Shan commented, raising his chopsticks. 'In this world of red dust, there's nothing but appearance, to which we give one name or another, as if it really existed or meant anything.'

'Masterfully said, our renowned Buddhist poet master,' Nameless responded. 'And that's why our abbot Stainless gave me this Buddhist name here. Name is nothing, and nameless is also nothing.'

Perhaps intrigued with their Zen-spirited talk, Nameless remained standing by the table, nodding respectfully like a private-room waiter in attendance, instead of immediately excusing himself.

'Our temple is known for its vegetarian meals,' he went on with another broad grin, 'much better known than the exotic dishes at Xuanji's wild parties.'

It was an unexpected comment from the young monk, who might have heard Xuanji's name mentioned earlier in the talk between Han Shan and Judge Dee. But why was he bringing it up?

While Han Shan might have told the judge what he knew about her life as a poetess, a young monk in the temple not too far from the nunnery could have known more about the case, particularly about the trial under the local mayor.

'You know what, Nameless, Han Shan and I were talking about poetry, but also about things happening here. And about Xuanji's murder case, too. She's an excellent poetess. Both Han Shan and I have read her poems. Her murder trial was so sensational that we cannot help feeling curious about it. You must have heard or seen a thing or two about it.'

'Oh, it's such a spectacular trial. I was lucky enough to be in the audience that succeeded in squeezing into the courtroom that morning.'

'You're lucky, indeed,' Judge Dee said, pulling out a chair for him. 'Sit at the table and tell us about it.'

Judge Dee had a feeling that, sitting across the table, Han Shan began to suspect the real motive of the judge's visit to the temple, but the poet monk was a wise man, simply nodding in encouragement, picking a slice of the vegetarian rice paddy eel, and sipping at his tea, without saying anything.

So Nameless seated himself at the table, poured out a cup of tea for himself, and launched into a vivid account of the trial with great gusto.

'That morning, when Xuanji was brought into the courtroom from prison, pale and disheveled and barefoot in black iron chains, what a shock it was to all of us at the courtroom! Not at all the beauty we had imagined.'

'What did she say to the mayor?'

'Instead of pleading guilty, she kept on saying that she did not know anything.'

'Did you know anything about the murder case before the trial, Nameless?'

'No, not really, except that the body of her maid Ning was discovered in the nunnery backyard on the third day of the month. According to Xuanji's statement, the day before, Ning had mentioned to her about going back home for a day or two, so Xuanji did not suspect anything about Ning's absence when she came back from shopping that afternoon. Being all alone in the nunnery, she started drinking by herself, tossing down one cup after another until she fell straight into a drunken stupor.

'Thereupon Mayor Pei summoned two witnesses who had been to the parties at the nunnery. They both testified that she's no alcoholic, hardly touching a drop at the parties. Still, she kept saying she was dead drunk that afternoon, unaware of anything that was happening around her at the time.'

'Was there any other evidence found in the nunnery or in the backyard?'

'That I don't know, Your Honor, but in accordance with a coroner's report, Ning was brutally beaten, kicked, and whipped until she breathed her last. The broken whip was also buried with her, I've heard.

'Anyway, Xuanji's statement about her ignorance did not add up. With all the evidence pointing to her, Mayor Pei had no choice but to interrogate her further in the courtroom, you know, with a brutal bludgeon beating.'

'A bludgeon beating of Xuanji in public!' Han Shan commented for the first time.

'Oh, what a scene in public! She's known as such a great

beauty. And an arrogant one, too. In the past, ordinary people like us could not even have dreamed of taking a close look at her. So we would not have missed it for the world. Now she was pinned down on the ground, with her pants pulled down to the ankles, and her bare buttocks glistening white like two half-moons, and part of her blouse pulled up, too—'

'Such a humiliation for a well-known poetess like Xuanji!' Han Shan cut in hastily.

'Things like that happen in the courtroom,' Judge Dee said, stroking his white-streaked beard. 'The moment a suspect – particularly a female one – is pinned down to the ground, with the constables raising the bludgeons high, and pulling down her pants, she may more likely than not start spilling out secrets, being too crushed even at the thought of the cruel humiliation.'

'You can say that again, Your Honor. How could she have ever held her head high again? There would be no way for her to live down the shame. Never. Do you think a man would touch her with the memories of her naked butt like a cracked watermelon, broken under the gaze of all the men standing around, watching like hungry wolves? She's definitely bewitched out of her mind, as people may tell you,' Nameless said enthusiastically, carried way with the vivid details of the courtroom scene, his cheeks flushed and his voice hoarse. 'Under the bludgeons, she writhed and screamed like a dying fox. After less than ten blows, her bare thighs and buttocks were already a bloody mess.

'Then they had to turn her over, spread-eagled on her back, her groin hairy, luxuriant like a black fox, and her bare thighs scarlet like *jinhua* hams—'

'So you were there, watching, all the time?' Judge Dee cut in before Nameless could have moved further.

'Yes, I was there, watching from the very beginning. Unfortunately, she passed out after fifteen blows or so and the constables had to stop.'

'She did not spill even under the blows?'

'No. No one could tell why, but she's finished, no question about it.' Nameless paused to chopstick up a plump and shiny red date fruit from a cold dish. 'Oh, it's our chef's special today, called the *soft heart.* With the kernel removed, the fruit is filled with sticky white rice and steamed in a bamboo steamer. Sweet, soft, and date-flavored.'

'Another interesting name,' Han Shan commented reflectively. 'The appearance of things in this world – you call it soft or hard.'

'Alas, I don't think our mayor has such a soft heart for a beauty like Xuanji. People do not believe he will ever let her off the hook so easily.'

'Why?'

'The mayor had invited her to a party at his residence, but she said no,' Nameless said, shaking his head again. 'At least, that's the story several people have told me. What a huge loss of face for the mayor! And what an opportunity for him to retaliate in the courtroom!'

'Come on. Declining a party invitation is not a big deal. How could the mayor have stooped to such a low level? It would not have helped his official reputation at all.' Judge Dee added after a pause, 'His name is Pei?'

'Yes, his name is Pei Changhong. And people are also speculating about the real reason behind it.'

'The real reason?'

'The mayor is also a man – a man rejected by a woman.'

'Rejected – you mean he fell for her?'

'He wanted her to come to the party not just as his guest, but as his woman. Everyone knows about it. Whether as his woman or his guest, however, it's very uncommon for a mayor to invite a courtesan home. And it appeared to be an extraordinary favor he was trying to do for her. But far from appreciating it, she gave a flat no to the invitation without any pretext. A loud slap on the face for him.'

'You're certainly very well informed, Nameless.'

'Our temple is frequented by celebrities, Your Honor, and they tell us things like that. Anyway, guess what happened then? Just a couple of days after the trial, she abruptly pleaded guilty in prison, coming up with an equally preposterous statement, which no one would buy. She insisted that she had been drunk that day, but not in a totally unconscious stupor as she had described in the courtroom. In the new version, later that afternoon, when her maid Ning talked back to her for something she could no longer remember, she flew into an uncontrollable rage. She beat Ning up with all her strength – without really knowing what she was doing – until to her horror, the maid-servant suddenly dropped dead to the floor. Panic-stricken, Xuanji managed to dig a large hole in the backyard and buried Ning there in a hurry under the cover of night.'

'That's strange,' Judge Dee said reflectively. 'Such a statement still spells the death sentence for her. Manslaughter. In other words, she suffered the brutal bludgeon beatings at the courtroom for nothing?'

'Well, imagine what could have happened to her then – a young, attractive woman alone in a dark, isolated prison cell, where horrible things have happened time and again – abusing, torturing, raping, and what not. Have you heard of those gruesome tortures, such as the wooden horse for a woman to ride bare-assed, riding non-stop with a hardwood wand bobbing up and down in her holes—'

'Stop there!' Han Shan cut in with an agitated voice. 'But how could she have possibly killed the maid without knowing anything about it?'

'It's all because of the black fox spirit,' Nameless said with a wry smile. 'She's fucked out of her brains!'

'For the majority of the local folk, they could not help attributing the murder case to the curse of the black fox spirit, as if that alone could have explained all the inexplicable facts in the mystery,' Judge Dee said, putting a steamed red date fruit of 'soft heart' into his mouth. The sticky rice tasted surprisingly sweet and delicious. 'Well, tell us something more about the legend of the black fox spirit, Nameless.'

'I'm a Buddhist monk, not a Daoist monk, Your Honor.'

'Humor us, please.' Judge Dee poured more water into the monk's cup in a gesture of appreciation.

Those fox spirit stories could have had their roots in Daoism, but Judge Dee wondered at the possible existence of a clear-cut dividing line between Buddhism and Daoism in the Tang Empire, especially among those village folks.

So the Buddhist monk began to recapture a popular folk belief about the fox spirit. According to it, an extremely lucky fox, perhaps one out of ten thousand, could have managed through supernatural cultivation or meditation to assume a human appearance, usually as a bewitching girl, for whom a young man would fall headlong like a moth into the fire, have his male essence sucked up in insatiable sex with her, and meet a tragic end before his time. Naturally, there are variations of the popular folk belief. A fox spirit could also take up the shape of a handsome young man and fuck a young woman out of her mind, out of shape – finally to a disastrous end.

'Nevertheless,' Nameless concluded, 'I have never heard of any tale about the fox spirit turning a pretty woman into a cold-blooded murderer.'

'Nor have I,' Han Shan said, echoing.

'Well, that's enough of the black or white fox spirits for one vegetarian meal, I think. You have told us a lot, Nameless, and I really appreciate it, but I have to discuss something with you, Han Shan,' Judge Dee said in a suddenly serious voice, tracing his finger on the table as if in an effort to write a character understandable to Han Shan alone. 'The murder case is so complicated because of possible involvement and pressure from above. What I'm going to tell you is supposed to be highly confidential, but I need the help of your profound wisdom, Han Shan.'

Judge Dee paused, eying Nameless without saying another word, picking up another sticky-rice-filled red date.

'It's indeed a fabulous meal from the temple kitchen.'

The young monk got the hint, rose with a bow, and withdrew respectfully from the room.

Tucking the silk scroll of Xuanji's calligraphy under his arm, Yang walked out of the curiosity store near the center of the town.

The village called Jiangling was in walking distance, also close to the Xianyi Nunnery. He decided to further his inquiries with Xuanji's neighbors first.

To his pleasant surprise, he found the scroll of her calligraphy provided him a ready pretext, and convincing evidence, as an antique dealer's servant inquiring for more business opportunities in the field.

As it turned out, however, the village people invariably avoided talking about Xuanji like the plague. With or without the pretext, mentioning her name seemed to be capable of bringing them bad luck because of the black fox spirit.

'Don't ever bring up her name to me. What an evil, shameless bitch! She ruins herself, the men around her, and the nunnery, too. An ominous black fox spirit indeed!'

'But have you ever seen a black fox spirit skulking around in the neighborhood?' Yang asked.

'A number of people have seen the damned black fox spirit in the neighborhood. Don't ask me any more questions about the evil bitch from hell.'

Another villager turned out to be even more dramatic in response.

'I have to spit three times on the ground for talking to you about the damned slut,' she said, spitting spitefully far more than three times and stamping her foot forcefully, too.

Spitting three times was a superstitious practice, Yang knew, for people to try to ward off evil spirits possibly lurking around them.

'A different question, then,' Yang said, changing his approach. 'Can you tell me something – if not about her – about the visitors to the nunnery?'

'She's simply evil incarnate, drawing those men to their dire ends. Some of them are rich and successful – you could tell by the number of servants following obsequiously behind them. Some were mysterious and well guarded. When they were with her, the village folk could hardly come close to the nunnery. Quite a few times, black-attired guards were seen patrolling around the front and the back doors of the nunnery.'

'Seriously! But can you tell me why?'

'She's such a notorious woman. For a visitor with high social status, it would not have done him any good if others bumped into the sight of the lascivious, notorious fox spirit moaning and groaning in his arms.'

'But how can those tall tales about the black fox spirit be so credible?'

'Of course they are real. I saw one with my own eyes.'

'When and where?'

'Near the backyard of the nunnery. Not long before the murder of that poor maid, I think. A black fox scurried over toward me in the dark night – near that particular corner of the nunnery backyard. No wonder the maid's body came to be buried there shortly afterward.'

'Interesting,' Yang said, thinking that it did not add up. How could the black fox have chosen to show others where the body was buried? If Xuanji really was the fox spirit incarnate, it was nothing short of suicidal.

According to some villagers, the movement of the fox spirit seemed to have intensified of late. Another mysterious catastrophic omen. Several neighbors swore that for the last one or two months, they saw the promiscuous animal skulking around the neighborhood numerous times.'

'What did they do about the black fox running amok all of a sudden?' Yang approached a bald, round-faced villager in threadbare clothes, who looked like a monk he had seen in the temple.

'What could they possibly do? They ran away helter-skelter at the sight of it. One of them swore on his mother's grave that it was a tall, monstrous, hairy black fox spirit walking straight toward him, baring its teeth.'

'Hold on. It was walking like a human being?'

'Yes, walking just like you and me. So people were really scared out of their wits. The abbess chose to leave the nunnery, I've heard, because of it.'

'Do you know where I can find the abbess?' Yang asked. 'Xuanji may have given something to the abbess when she moved in, I would say.'

'How can I possibly know the whereabouts of the frightened abbess? You're asking questions just like a neighborhood coordinator. If you're truly interested in cheap yet good antiques, you may well step in and take a good look at the bronze urn in my pigsty. Some people say it's handed down from the ancient Zhou Dynasty.'

Yang thanked him without going into the pigsty for a look at the bronze urn, and moved to another villager, and then to still another.

However, they hardly offered anything new or useful for the

investigation, except for some more intriguing details about the omnipresent black fox spirit, as if by way of explanation of the inexplicable mystery surrounding the murder case.

Could that be useful to Judge Dee? Yang started wondering about the possibility of Judge Dee's representing a black fox spirit scenario to Minister Wu, claiming that it was a generally accepted scenario in the neighborhood of the nunnery. Whatever political factors might have been involved, that would probably prove to be an apolitical one.

After Nameless left the temple room, Han Shan raised the teacup to Judge Dee with a smile. 'Now we are alone, you may discuss all the confidential details of the case with me, my celebrated Judge Dee. I'm no judge, but the murder case has become such a hot topic. Almost all the people I have met here over the last several days could not stop talking about Xuanji and the black fox spirit.'

'The case is very complicated, but I'm not serving as a judge here. I'm leaving for my new post, as you know. Last night, however, I received a request from Minister Wu to take a quick look into it. So I cannot help being curious about the case, which may also have a bearing on the collection of Xuanji's poems.'

'Don't worry about it, Judge Dee. Whatever we're discussing in the temple – about the poetry collection or the murder case – stays in the temple. Just between you and me.'

'Thank you, Han Shan. Now, to begin with, it's an open question as to whether Xuanji is a murderer or a victim in a devilish trap, as suggested in her original statement.'

'So you mean the body of the maid Ning was planted in the nunnery backyard by somebody else – with Xuanji being completely unconscious in a drunken stupor. But who could have planted the body and why, Judge Dee?'

'Xuanji's a much-sought-after celebrity courtesan, yet also arrogant in her way, as Nameless has just said. It's not unimaginable that she had made things unpleasant for some people – like her refusal to come to Mayor Pei's party.'

'It's possible,' Han Shan said, a finger massaging at his temple, 'but could that have been enough for such a murderous plot?'

'Do you think her "poetry talk" – night after night with one man or another – was something tolerable to the people intimately close to her – such as Wen or Zi'an?'

'That's a good question, Your Honor. The motive of intense jealousy. But both Wen and Zi'an have alibis, I happen to know. For the last two or three months, Wen has been sick and bedridden at home, hundreds of miles away. It would have been out of the question for him to travel all the way here. As for Zi'an, he's having a good time in a promising official position in another province, along with his wife and a baby on the way. I don't see how either of them could have chosen to set a trap against Xuanji at the moment.'

'You surely have a point, Han Shan.'

'Besides, it was Wen who pushed her into Zi'an's arms, and then it was Zi'an who pushed her into others' arms, so to speak. According to people in the circle, neither Wen nor Zi'an had been embarrassed or upset by her being a fashionably notorious courtesan here. And the three of them have kept on writing romantic poems for one another. No, I cannot see the motive in either of them.'

'It is so helpful to talk to you, Han Shan, with all your information in the circle of poets. I, too, do not believe they would have done that, but it could have taken me much longer to rule out that possibility. I have to read more of their poems, I think.'

'Wen has recently composed a nice *ci* poem for her,' Han Shan said. 'It would be fantastic for you to include the poem in the collection. You may add a note about the date of its composition. I'll find it for you. But back to the murder case at the present moment: is such a conspiracy theory backed up by any concrete evidence?'

'No, nothing concrete. But there seem to be too many coincidences. That guest of hers, for instance, who walked straight out to the spot in the backyard where the body of the maid was buried, still fresh and recognizable underneath the thin layer of soil. And that very guest who happened to know the people at Mayor Pei's office, who immediately dispatched runners to investigate in the nunnery. Also, the hue and cry about the flies circling the backyard corner was not even mentioned once in the case report regarding the crime scene.'

'But all this is just circumstantial, isn't it? As for the flies, they could have flown away by the time the runners went to the backyard.' Han Shan resumed after a short pause, 'Besides, for a set-up scenario like that, it would not have worked unless all the conditions were met. Xuanji had to stay inside the temple without being aware of anything outside during the time period when Ning was killed and buried; and that particular guest had to come out to the very spot in the backyard the next day, and in the company of other guests – for the hue and cry to reach the mayor who then had to take immediate action. In other words, for such an elaborate plot, the conspirator had to be someone who was resourceful and desperate.'

'That's true, but one of those big bugs rejected by her could have been sufficiently resourceful and desperate.'

'Well, it sounds like an echo of what Nameless said about Mayor Pei, Judge Dee. Still, I want to say something about Pei. He had told me about his invitation to Xuanji long before the murder case.'

'What did he say to you – and when?'

'It was when I first came to stay at the temple here. A couple of months ago. Mayor Pei paid me a visit, saying he wanted to have a party for poets and writers at his official residence. Xuanji was also on the invitation list because he thought she had been treated badly by a distant cousin of his – none other than Zi'an's wife. He wanted to do something for her as a way of compensation, but she flatly declined the invitation. So it had nothing whatever to do with any romantic inclination. Gossip and misinterpretations of this kind of thing could have spread, however, like uncontrollable wild weeds.

'And then, as Mayor Pei happened to be the one in charge of the trial, it's natural for people like Nameless to speculate. But was there anything improper in the way Mayor Pei treated her during the trial? I cannot tell, but you may judge objectively as an experienced judge yourself.'

'Conventionally, if a suspect does not confess,' Judge Dee said, shaking his head slightly, 'the mayor or magistrate is justified to have him or her beaten for twenty or thirty blows in the courtroom. In her case, some consideration could have been shown for a young female celebrity like Xuanji. Such humiliation in public. But I don't see how Mayor Pei could fit into a plot or retaliation scenario. With her rejection of his party invitation known to quite a number of people, it would be easy for them to accuse him of persecuting her for an undisclosed reason. He should have known better. Even after she pleaded guilty in prison, some people would still proclaim that "she was tortured into confession." It's a tight spot for him. No matter how unconvincing her confession sounded, he could hardly afford to give her another beating in public for the reasons we've just discussed.'

'But how do you think he is going to proceed?'

'I don't know. The scenario of Xuanji being the murderer is not compelling, either. I simply cannot see her motive for the murder of a maidservant. Nor did she have the physical strength for it.'

'On that I agree with you, Judge Dee. How could a willowy girl like Xuanji have killed and buried someone all by herself? With those questions you've mentioned, it may be difficult to close the case simply on the basis of her confession.'

'Under normal circumstance, the moment a confession was made, the case would have been submitted to the higher authorities for approval, and the criminal would then be punished accordingly. But with her being such a celebrity, and with men of letters making a petition for her . . .'

'So that's how Minister Wu came to you?'

'Wu wants a quick conclusion to the case, I suppose, but at the same time, it has to be one acceptable to the people. That could mean, among other things, Wu believes there may be something or somebody else involved in the case.'

'But why should people like Minister Wu have been so anxious about it?'

'That I don't know. There are more things in heaven and earth, Han Shan, than are dreamed of in your poetry.'

'That's truly beyond me, Judge Dee. Just one more question. What do you think of those tall tales about the black fox spirit?'

'Again, I don't know. I can hardly see its connection to the murder case. At least not for the moment. Confucius says, "A gentleman doesn't talk about ghosts and spirits." But in the absence of any other possible clue, I may as well take a look into that, too.

'Now, one of the first questions a judge has to ask himself is "Who could have benefited from the murder?" Surely not a black fox spirit – especially if the spirit and Xuanji are one and the same. But I also have a question for you, Han Shan. Is there anything else unusual you have seen or heard in connection to the nunnery?'

'It's a Buddhist temple here, and the nunnery is a Daoist one. I've never been to the nunnery, not a single time, even though it's not too far away. Now you mention it, I think I may have heard of something. According to a monk here, there were a couple of mysterious men seen moving around in the vicinity of the nunnery, and they prevented neighbors from coming close to it.'

'Was that before the murder case or after?'

'Before, but for any details, you may need to talk to Mayor Pei. Sorry, I cannot help you any more than that.'

'The discussion with you has already helped such a lot, Han Shan.'

'Last night, I was rereading *Diamond Sutra*. What an enlightening book indeed! Everything under the sun cannot but be appearance. We cannot see through the appearance because we put too much of ourselves into it. The same can probably be said about your investigation. About the black fox spirit, too. I'll get a copy for you if you have not read it.'

'That will be fantastic. I appreciate it from the bottom of my heart, Han Shan.'

Stepping out of the village, Yang found himself being an investigation assistant who would not rest content with the black fox spirit scenario. Nor was it likely, he knew, for his master to swallow such an explanation. As a long-time servant to Judge Dee, he believed he had to do something more.

So he turned back and managed to locate the 'neighborhood coordinator office' at the roadside near the entrance of the village. A middle-aged man surnamed Bao with a receding hairline and a large beard was in charge of the small office. A neighborhood coordinator was a nobody in the Tang official system, though not without some real controlling and surveilling power over people in the neighborhood, and a small stipend from the mayor's office as well.

Yang approached Bao with a modified pretext that he was a servant to a wealthy businessman dabbling in the collection of calligraphy and paintings, and that he was running around in search of anything Xuanji might have left behind that could be potentially valuable. It took him little time to succeed in inviting Bao out for a cup at a shabby eatery by the roadside.

They turned out to be the only customers there at that time of the day. Sitting at a rough wooden table with the village in view, Yang poured out a cup of yellow rice wine for Bao and handed him a tiny piece of silver.

'In our line of business, background information can turn out to be extremely helpful. A piece of junk Xuanji left behind somewhere may prove to be worth a huge fortune, considering those wealthy patrons of hers. That's why what you can tell me matters such a lot. Things like what she did the day the body of the maid was discovered in the backyard, or the day before . . .'

'Surely you're a very capable servant for your master, Yang. And I am the very man for your inquiry; that much I can assure you,' Bao said, pocketing the small piece of silver readily. 'In fact, Mayor Pei asked me about those things, too, though I don't know anything about his interests in the collection of brush pen calligraphy and paintings. So I have done quite an extensive investigation of it.'

'Really! That's fantastic. But for me, it's just an investigation for business.'

'Well, investigation is investigation. I like your way of trying your best to do a good job of it,' Bao said, taking up a piece of fried fish fillet in yellow wine sauce. 'It's excellent wine. To your business successes!'

After three cups of the mellow yet strong rice wine, Bao became a bit tipsy; his tongue was loosened, and his face animated and flushed like the crest of a cock when it's ready to jump into the fighting ring.

'Xuanji had good stuff from those rich and powerful men dancing around her. As neighborhood watchers, we may not be high on the social ladder, but we have the important responsibility to surveil all the time, so we may report anything and everything to the higher authorities. Our job is truly crucial to the maintenance of the political stability of the Great Tang Empire. No one in the neighborhood can escape our watchful eyes. And I can assure you, Yang, she got much more from those rich and powerful visitors than mere calligraphies or paintings. How? I don't think you need me to tell you.'

'The rich and powerful visitors must have been buzzing around her like flies smelling and sucking blood, I guess.'

'What an insightful, ironical metaphor indeed! She was caught because of the flies whirling around the blood in the nunnery backyard. Karma! So that's quite a story for another cup, right?' Bao said with increasing gusto, crunching the soft-boiled chicken foot, and reaching out to fill his cup again. 'In short, she's a promiscuous slut. Shamelessly carrying on with one big bug after another, she took it for granted that they would continue to shower money and jewels and antiques – and protection, too – on her forever.'

'She must have lost her mind.'

'Fucked out of her mind, I tell you! Apart from those fly-like visitors, the people in the neighborhood have been so fed up with her wild, infamous ways, but it was not merely a disgrace to the village. It could also lead to political disaster for the whole country.'

'What do you mean, Bao?'

'According to a governmental document available to neighborhood coordinators at my level, quite a number of old-fashioned scholars in the capital saw her as a representative of the current moral decline of the Tang Empire. Whatever they could not have said against the empress in the open, they said out loud and clear through the Xuanji case.'

'Yes, these things could have been complicated in the Tang Empire. But no politics over the cups, Bao. The steamed live carp is not bad. It tastes so tender and fresh. Have a piece more. Now let me ask you a different question. Why should Xuanji have killed the maid?'

'Because she's so bewitched. And, more likely than not, the maid was bewitched, too. About ten days ago, a villager saw a young woman kneeling stark naked in front of the nunnery, her head hung low, her face covered in long black hair, and her bare back glistening with sweat and crisscrossed welts,' Bao went on, taking another large gulp, licking his lips voraciously, and squinting his eyes as if surveilling the very scene. 'When he tried to take a better look, however, it turned out to be a black fox kneeling there, kowtowing to the full bright moon like crazy, and vanishing into the air the next moment.'

Once again, the evil of the black fox spirit came to serve as the infallible interpretation of the bizarre murder case. Yang smothered a sigh, stuffing into his mouth a large fatty chunk of pork braised in red soy sauce.

'The villager must have heard so many fox spirit stories that he perhaps imagined things in the depth of the night,' Yang said, waving his hand in dismissal of the hallucination as he changed the subject. 'By the way, please tell me something about Wei. People told me he may have things – valuable things – from Xuanji. I'm just wondering whether it would be worth my while to contact him.'

'Wow, you have heard of Wei, too! Let me tell you what. He's an impossible gigolo, and he sucked her dry like a leech. In fact, the place he stays in was also bought with her money, a wooden hut fairly close to the nunnery, so he could have easily sneaked over to her at night. People say she's simply bewitched by him.'

'You mean he is the black fox spirit?'

'Who knows? There are both male and female fox spirits in this red-dust world of ours. No one can tell for sure. I don't know too much about Wei, but if you want, you may talk to a flower girl surnamed Zhang or Zhan. She's a sort of a confidante for Xuanji. Her flower garden is located near the southern end of the village. She sent flowers to Xuanji regularly for her parties, and Xuanji or Wei occasionally went to her flower garden to pick up the orders, too. She surely can tell you much more about him. And about her as well. Most of the neighbors here did not want to mix with Xuanji or

Wei, but that flower girl was an exception. Xuanji's a very valuable customer for her.'

'That's true.'

'I don't have her address, but you don't have to worry about it. You just need to ask the village people there for the flower girl. She's just another young fox spirit like Xuanji.'

'How?'

'Young girls like her should not have mixed with people in public. In the time-honored Confucian tradition, they should stay at home and wait for an arranged marriage. She lost her parents when she was just a teenager, and she turned into a flower girl. Indeed, they are young fox spirits of the same-colored hair.'

Enough of hearsay about the fox spirits for one meal, Yang contemplated, and he failed to see anything wrong with a young girl struggling to support herself. He raised the last question over the cup. 'Just one more question. Xuanji's a renowned poetess. How can I obtain a copy of her poems? It's for my master, who is an impossible bookworm.'

'You may try your luck at the local temple market fair, but it's still more than a month away – I mean the next market fair. For the moment, though,' Bao said with a wine-sodden hiccup, 'you may contact a typesetter/printer surnamed Mo in the town, who did a limited edition for her, I've heard. For reasons beyond me, the mayor also asked me about her poetry collections. There must be a lot of bookworms under the Tang Dynasty sun.'

'That would be very helpful – the address of the typesetter, I mean.'

'Here it is. It's not too far away.'

'Thank you so much, Bao. I'm afraid I have to run a couple more errands for my master, but you can take your time finishing the wine.'

Yang copied Mo's address, paid the bill, and left the eatery with the neighborhood coordinator still burying his head in the leftovers on the table.

Again, Yang hurried back to the town, like tumbleweed rolling in the wind, and he started to feel weary with the trips back and forth between the village and the town.

Luckily, it was not too much effort to find Mo, the typesetter/printer/publisher in question.

Mo was a shrewd-looking businessman in his early sixties, who did not even ask Yang why he wanted a copy of Xuanji's poems.

'Yes, I did a limited edition for her,' Mo said. 'It's titled *Night Poetry Talk*, but she took away all the copies. No more than one hundred of them.'

'Such a small number?'

'It's for her men only – I mean, those special visitors to the nunnery – so the poems were written with their names mentioned in the titles, in the texts, or in the notes about the occasions of those poems. Most of the poems in the edition are fairly amorous. Not necessarily that explicit, to be fair to her. She gave them her signed copies as souvenirs – something for them to brag and boast about, and for those who had not yet had poems dedicated to them, they would hope that she might also come to write for them like that in the future. As a result, they went on showering money or gifts on her for the unique favor. After all, poetry is for thousands of autumns, and they believed their names would last forever in her lines. In the meantime, it further spread the name of her poetry parties in the nunnery. A very clever practice, I have to say, and it's worth all the money she spent on printing.'

'I see. But you may have a way of getting hold of a copy for me, I believe. I'll pay you double the price for it.'

'It's not for sale,' Mo said, waving his hand, and eying Yang with a suggestion of suspicion. 'She took all of them, as I have just told you. It may only be a matter of time, however, before we have a reprint at the conclusion of the sensational case. A much larger print run, perhaps with some profit for me. Then I will be able to sell you a copy.'

Mo must have taken him for another in the publishing business, and he did not like the prospect of a copy of the earlier edition falling into the hand of a potential rival.

'To tell the truth,' Yang said, thinking that he had no choice but to play his trump card, 'I'm here for my bookish master who is not interested in your line of business. He's simply a fan of her poems, but at the same time, it's also because of the murder case that he wants to read her poems.'

'Who is he?'

'Dee Renjie.'

'Judge Dee! You should have told me earlier,' Mo said, rising in a hurry to reach into a black-painted chest behind him and take a folder out of it. 'I do not have a single copy left, that's true, but I still have the proof of her poetry collection.'

'The proof. That's incredible.'

'Sure enough, here it is. The very proof. And His Honor may keep it as long as he likes, of course. He is such a noble Confucianist statesman of integrity, unwavering in his support of the Li family in the difficult times. Yes, Judge Dee can have it. No charge for him.'

'Thank you so much, Mr Mo. My master will truly appreciate it, but you may still need the proof for your reprint edition.'

'I have another copy – in my own poor handwriting, hardly readable to others. It's really an honor for Judge Dee to have the proof from me. Let me wrap it for you, Yang.'

'A different question, Mr Mo. Since you're familiar with Xuanji, did you happen to notice anything unusual about her in the days before the discovery of the maid's body in the nunnery backyard?'

'It's for the murder investigation, correct? But I was not that familiar with her – except in the matter of book business, as you know.'

'But you've just mentioned that she put the names of her lovers into the poems. What about them?'

'Yes, Wen and Zi'an particularly. Wen is one of the most prominent contemporary poets, both in *shi* and *ci*. A number of masterpieces in the "soft style" – even with a female persona like her. It's to her credit that she had included her poems written to him in the collection. As for Zi'an, you know the love story between the two. In spite of his success in the capital civil service examination, he's a mediocre poet with hardly anything readable except for two or three quatrains written in response to hers. But neither Wen nor Zi'an has been here for at least half a year . . .'

Mo gushed on like the bookish man he truly was, but the talk about poetry-writing and printing began to wear Yang out.

'For a woodblock printer like me, she's an extraordinary customer. Not too many poets could have afforded to have their poems printed like her.'

Mo then took out a block of wood engraved with all the tiny Chinese characters.

'It's just for one page, you see, but it took me several days to have all the words engraved. A couple of mistakes could have ruined the whole block. So most poets prefer to hire a calligrapher for handwritten copies. It's a lot cheaper that way.'

'Yes, I see.'

'She paid me well. And she introduced both Wen and Zi'an to me. In the event of printing Wen's poetry collection, it will be read for thousands of years because of my special edition, you know, so it's an incredible opportunity I cannot afford to miss, not just for the money.'

Yang felt increasingly lost. As he was not a poetry reader, what Mo was talking about meant little to him. But could that be of any help to Judge Dee? Stealing a look out of the lattice window, he saw the sky overhead becoming somber with rain clouds scurrying across the horizon.

He rose, thanked Mo, and left with the proof clutched tightly in his hand.

After an exchange of pleasantries with several other monks in the courtyard, after admiration of the poems left by other celebrated poets on the garden wall, after inquiries about the possibility of having a service arranged at short notice, after casual questions about the interesting or unusual things that had happened of late around the temple, Judge Dee had just arrived back at his room, putting his black cap on the table, when Yang hurried in with a package in his hand.

Yang appeared to be in high spirits, in spite of his rain-dampened clothes.

'You got caught in the rain?'

'It's just a drizzle. Nothing to worry about. Here is the proof of the collection *Night Poetry Talk* by Xuanji.'

'You've actually obtained the proof, Yang?'

Yang took the seat opposite, drained a cup of tea in one gulp, and told Dee what he had learned about Xuanji during the day.

The account Yang gave was far from well organized, digressing with details seemingly irrelevant to the murder case, especially with those tall tales about the black fox spirit he had learned of in the village. It was quite a while before Yang came to the end of his excited narration.

'In addition, here is a silk scroll of Xuanji's poem in her own calligraphy. It was sold to the store by someone named Wei, a man she had been seeing in secret, though it's hardly a secret in the neighborhood.'

'It's a steal for the price you paid.'

'I thought you might need me for something else in the temple, so I did not have time go to see the flower girl. She's at the southern end of the village. Perhaps I can have a talk with her tomorrow.'

'A marvelous job you have done today!' Judge Dee said, rubbing his hands over the top of the proof. 'I truly appreciate it. Now it's time for you to take a break. I'll have the temple special – a bowl of mushroom soup noodles – delivered to your room. It's delicious. You deserve it after such a long, productive day's work.'

Yang looked up at his master, making no comment. He knew better than to push for some immediate response regarding the investigation from Judge Dee, who kept caressing the silk scroll spread out on the table, without offering to tell him anything about what he had learned from Han Shan in the temple.

After having finished the second cup of lukewarm tea, Yang rose, bowed, and withdrew like a respectful attendant, though he had hardly any appetite for the celebrated vegetarian soup noodles back in his room.

Alone, Judge Dee began reading the proof of Xuanji's poetry collection in the temple room. It was so peaceful, except for occasional rustles of falling leaves in the backyard.

He did not know how long he had been lost in the world of her poems. The temple bell was carrying the dusk over in a light breeze when he looked up from the proof, rubbing his strained eyes, toward a small green bamboo grove swaying gently outside the lattice window.

There were about forty poems in all in the proof, with the changes and notes made and marked by the poetess herself. Something immensely valuable if he had truly been such a collector as represented by Yang in the village.

Most of them were love poems, though readable in an allegorical way, too. There were quite a number of them that Judge Dee was reading for the first time.

After the long talk with Han Shan earlier in the day, Judge Dee thought he was in a better position to read more into those sad and sentimental lines composed by Xuanji.

And it might be a workable idea for him, Judge Dee reflected, to have two collections compiled instead of one, as Han Shan had suggested. One, the complete poems of Xuanji, and the other, the love poems of Xuanji – possibly with her love poems as well as some others written to her in response included in the same collection – and that with detailed biographical notes. In the meantime, there could have been some new, uncollected pieces recently discovered as those for the proof from Mo had been delivered about a year before.

Whether Judge Dee could afford the time or the energy for either of the collections, he hastened to remind himself, would be another story.

Halfway through the proof, he came practically to rule out Wen and Zi'an as possible suspects in connection to the murder case. It was not just because of their alibis. More because of the fact that these poems actually appealed to the vanity of her ex-lovers to have such a celebrated poetess, Judge Dee read on with knitted brows, complain in her poems that she was pining away, missing them in sleepless nights. The world of appearance is nothing if not informed with self-centered vanity, as Han Shan had observed. Neither Wen nor Zi'an had a motive, apparently, for a devious plot against her.

It was getting dark outside. Lighting a candle, Judge Dee came across another 'personal poem' titled 'To a Girl in the Neighborhood,' which reminded him of what Yang had told him about the flower girl in the village.

You cover your face with the silk sleeves,
bashful in the sunlight, too languid
to apply make-up in the worries
of the springtime. Alas, it is easier
to find an extremely valuable treasure
than a true-hearted lover.
Weeping against the tear-soaked pillow
at night, you suffer a heartbreak
walking in the midst of the flowers.
With a handsome talent like Song Yu
beside you, why should you feel bitter
about a cold-hearted Wang Chang?

According to the information gathered by Yang, Xuanji did not have any friends in the neighborhood except the flower girl surnamed Zhang. Both the textual and the contextual pointed to the flower girl in question, but at the same time, the poem pointed more to Xuanji herself. It was conventional for people to express themselves through a poem seemingly addressed to another. With the two men mentioned at the end of the poem – Song Yu and Wang Chang – both known as handsome men and gifted writers – the poem actually read more like self-encouragement. The mentioning of 'a cold-hearted Wang Chang' at the end of the poem came with an implied disparagement of Wen or Zi'an. After all, she had some other young, handsome talents available to her in those 'poetry talks' at the nunnery, so why should she feel so inconsolable about her situation?

Putting aside the proof, Judge Dee found his mind bogged down in the sentimental lines. He was not a poet on a par with Xuanji. Taking a sip of the cold tea, he stroked his gray beard with a sigh.

For a break from the poetry, he decided to work his way through the list of the possible contacts Yang had obtained for him. The next day, he was going to start with the flower girl in question, who was called by her neighbors 'another young fox spirit like Xuanji.' And the typesetter/publisher of the poetry collection, who appeared to be quite knowledgeable about the literature circle Xuanji had moved in. And the bookstore owner, who had a scroll of Xuanji's poem in her own calligraphy. And then Wei, who had the poem copied out to him . . . but possibly after Judge Dee had talked to all other contacts.

The list of names turned out to be quite long. He wondered whether he would be able to approach all of them in one day.

After circling a couple more names, he put down the list, He felt inexplicably tired, rubbing his temples.

Looking out of the paper window, he could hardly see anything in the temple courtyard, though a lone monk's scripture-chanting was heard in a barely audible monotone. Probably something about the vanity of human passion in the world of red dust, the chanting went on in a broken rhythm to the night watchman's insistent knocker beating along the trail outside the temple.

He pushed open the window. The night was quite advanced. Across the deep-blue sky, the moon began setting as if perched on a gigantic black crow's wing – as ominous as the black fox spirit in those folk tales. There is nothing but the appearance from one's own perspective at this time, in this place. He sighed, having spent almost half a night reading through those poems and speculating about the contacts for the murder investigation.

The flickering candle gave out an unexpected sparkle. What omen could it have spelled for Xuanji? She was staying in a dark prison cell, probably with no candle at her side.

He snuffed the candle clumsily with his fingers, thinking he might finally be ready to go to bed.

THREE

Judge Dee stepped out of the temple in the early morning, taking a deep inhale of the fresh air in the blue hills. It had rained in the night. A touch of green was seen stretching out toward the distant gray horizon. He still felt tired, yawning, when he saw Yang come striding over.

'I'm taking a walk around the neighborhood this morning, Yang. Possibly quite a long walk, I think. So you'll have a free day for yourself here.'

'The hill trail might be quite steep and slippery this morning, Master. What about having a sedan chair arranged for you?'

'No. I need to stretch my legs a little. It will be just a leisurely stroll. I'm not that old yet.'

'If you say so, Master. In the meantime, is there anything else for me to do about the Xuanji case?'

'No, we're just taking a look into it, but not doing any real investigation for Minister Wu. As a matter of fact, you have already done more than enough for the investigation. For a change, stay here today, and enjoy the enchanting view and the fabulous vegetarian food of the temple.'

'Yes, Master,' Yang said, bowing low like an obedient servant, 'whatever you say.'

Sometimes a man chooses to play a role for reasons not necessarily clear to himself, but after a while, the role starts to play him instead, consciously or not. That perhaps applied, however, only to the one side of Yang, who was not just an obedient servant but also a stubborn, self-declared investigation assistant, unwilling to give up that role so easily, Judge Dee reflected.

Wasn't that also a self-reflection of Dee himself, the so-called Judge Dee, he wondered, smiling a wry smile.

A flash of the morning light on the wings of a surprised blue jay surprised him out of his reveries.

* * *

It took some effort for Judge Dee to make his way down, stepping carefully along the narrow, slippery trail winding down from the mid-hill temple, which overlooked a green expanse of rice paddy fields at the foot of the hill.

A tiny pine nut was heard dropping in the secluded trail, with the bell from the temple growing fainter in a cool breath of wind. The view was largely wrapped in a somber opaqueness of the morning mist. The tall dew-speckled weeds along both sides of the tranquil hill trail glistened, off and on, like myriads of curious eyes blinking inquisitively.

It did not take too long for Judge Dee to find his blue cotton gown sweat-drenched, as he kept trudging on along the trail. He was growing old, he told himself, fastening his straw hat against the morning sun.

He came in view of the village, a medium-sized one with small yet colorful houses scattered around in the neighborhood of the nunnery.

At the village entrance, he approached the villagers to ask about the flower girl in question. An elderly man directed him to the flower garden, merely raising a bony finger with a suggestion of annoyance.

So, at the southern end of the village, he saw a small flower garden with green bamboo fences circling around, in which a young girl in homespun indigo was watering a row of flowerpots near the garden door. It turned out to be none other than Zhang, perhaps no more than sixteen or seventeen, whose hands were soiled with garden work. So were her bare feet.

Not at all like a seductive fox spirit in those tall folk tales, she looked up at Dee, smiling a shy smile and lowering her head in a demure way.

But it was perhaps not too surprising, Judge Dee observed, that she had earned for herself the epithet of 'another fox spirit' in the company of Xuanji.

The official Tang discourse regarding the future of young girls was that of arranged marriage. Because of it, they usually chose to present themselves in public as little as possible. They were not supposed to be involved in any prenuptial romance, as marriage had to be a matter arranged by their parents with the help of matchmakers. Anything that contradicted the time-honored tradition would be condemned and denounced in the light of the orthodox Confucian classics. For Zhang, a young girl who had to support herself by working in the flower shop, and eventually find a man by taking the matter in her own hands, she could not but be seen by others as a different, or even slutty, 'fox spirit' like Xuanji.

'I'm a poetry publisher,' Judge Dee said to her, coming straight to the point. 'I feel so sorry about what has happened to your friend Xuanji. I'm trying to compile a poetry collection for her. That's the least a bookish old admirer like me can do. I've just learned that you two saw each other quite a lot. Surely she has been more than a regular customer here for your flowers.'

'Yes, she came to my shop from time to time, but first and foremost as a customer for my flowers.'

'You don't have to be so modest about that. In fact, you're the very one in her poem titled "To a Girl in the Neighborhood," right? That speaks volumes about your friendship. It's a wonderful poem, which will be read for hundreds and hundreds of years, I can assure you of that.'

'Yes, that's the poem she wrote for me after one of her visits to the flower garden.'

'As a publisher, I believe it's important to get as much biographical information as possible about the poems. Particularly for a poetess like her. For instance, I can add a note about the inspiration she got from her visit to your garden. About what the two of you discussed. All that can turn out to be so helpful for readers to understand the poem. Some of the earlier annotated editions of her poems may not be accurate or reliable in that aspect, and it's crucial for a publisher like me to check and double-check.'

'It's a worthy project, sir. I'm just a poor, barely educated flower girl. For all her beauty and talent, she has condescended to talk to me occasionally about her poems, and I feel so grateful to her. I'll try to answer your questions the best I can.'

'How about telling me whatever you know about her daily life?'

Then the flower girl started giving him a detailed account of Xuanji's life after she had moved to the nunnery.

It was true that Xuanji frequently came to the flower garden because of the flowers she needed for her parties, but, from time to time, it was also because of their talking about and discussing the problems they had in common. They were young, single, and lonely, and both of them were seen as unorthodox. More so in Xuanji's case. In spite of the dominant Confucian discourse of arranged marriage, paradoxically, the early Tang Dynasty also happened to be a period when romantic affairs among young people could also be considered fashionable, at least in popular stories and poems. That made things harder for Xuanji, who felt helplessly trapped in the nunnery despite all her fancy parties and celebrated friends. That was not at all what she had dreamed of for her life. She was worried that she would soon lose her youth and beauty. And then everything else. As for those men at the parties, she knew clearly they cared only for her body – and even that only for the moment. She prayed that someone would come to rescue her from her plight, but for her, he had to be a man of higher social status. A knight in shining armor on a white horse, so to speak.

'A knight or not, has she had a "true-hearted lover" as described in that poem she wrote for you?' Judge Dee cut in with a question.

Zhang hesitated, leaning over a dainty pot of pale-pink peonies, keeping herself busy watering the flowers as an excuse for not responding to the question, and touching the petals with her nervous fingers.

Judge Dee lifted his gown and produced a tiny silver ingot from an inner pocket, weighing it in his hand.

'It's not a profitable business to publish poetry, but I'm a devoted fan, willing to go all out for the project because I believe, no matter what may happen to her, those poems of hers will live on for generations. For that, I need to know as much as possible about the background of the poems. The peonies are so lovely. Please send a bouquet of them to her on my behalf.'

'It's so kind of you, sir. Xuanji really loves peonies. She has even written a poem about them, but a bouquet does not take that much silver, sir.'

'Don't worry about it. You keep the change.'

'You're a very generous man,' she said, accepting the silver ingot. 'About your question regarding a "true-hearted lover" of hers, she once imagined she had a man who really cared for her, she told me.'

'Who?'

'Wei.'

'Wei – I think I've heard of that name before, but what do you mean by "once"?'

'Wei's a musician, young, handsome, and talented in his way, and he set a couple of her poems to music. At first she was crazy about him, but he was as poor as a rat, with no social or literary status to speak of. What's worse, it did not take too long for her to be devastated with the discovery that he's good for nothing – except in her bed. And for that matter, possibly in other women's beds, too.'

'But she continued to see him?'

'He denied those allegations, but she too was seeing other men. So theirs turned into a sort of open relationship. He was not the one for her, she realized, but she nonetheless kept him with a kind of tacit understanding between the two of them. Whenever she was not seeing other men, he would sneak over to her from the small hut she had bought for him – or, occasionally, for a change, she would scurry over to him under the cover of darkness. In short, she continued to see him, even though she no longer regarded him as a serious choice – definitely not as a "true-hearted lover."'

'Wei must have had some idea about the other man or men she was seeing before the murder?'

'It's possible. But why the question?'

'For a better understanding of her works. The occasions for the composition of her poems. Reading her poems, the readers may have a vague impression about the other men she had been seeing, and they are curious for details. For instance, what do you know about Wen, and for that matter Zi'an, too?'

'I don't know too much about Wen. They wrote passionate love poems for each other, some of which she showed me. Indeed, she's very proud of his poems to her. Had Wen cared that much for her, however, he would not have pushed her into the arms of another man. At least that's what I think.'

'It's true,' Judge Dee agreed.

'As for Zi'an, he's simply a hen-pecked, false-hearted coward. I saw him just once in the neighborhood of the nunnery. It was at the time she first moved over here. She had since become so disappointed with him. As far as I know, he has hardly written to her since his departure for his official position in another province in the company of his wife.'

Judge Dee had not expected too much new information from that direction, so he shifted to questioning about what Xuanji did on the day of the murder.

'No, I did not see Xuanji the day that one of her guests discovered the body in the nunnery backyard. The third day of the month, I remember. If anything, I don't think they were important guests to her. She usually did not have lunch parties except for those who happened to drop in. Those visitors came on the pretext of sightseeing around the nunnery. Xuanji did not order any flowers from me that day.'

'No, I mean the day before. The maid was killed the previous day. The second day of the month.'

'Oh, that day, I did see Xuanji. Around noon-time, I think, she came over to pick up some flowers. Expensive bouquets of peonies, her favorite flower, most likely for a special guest in the evening—'

'Hold on, Zhang. You mentioned that she once wrote a poem about the peony. I don't think I have read that poem.'

'It's little wonder. She composed it only about two months ago. That day, after buying a large pot of pink peonies, she talked to me for quite a while, and then dashed off these lines in praise of the peony.'

'What did she talk about to you on that occasion?'

'Mostly about the peony. She told me that it's the national flower of the Tang Empire, but the empress would have chosen another flower because of her uncontrollable ambition. Another empire and another national flower. Sometimes Xuanji said things I don't really understand.'

That went beyond the flower because of the politics involved in the background. The empress wanted to have another flower named as the national flower. Her suggestion came as a test of people's reaction to her plan to change the Tang Empire to the Zhou Empire. A number of high-ranking officials opposed the idea, including Judge Dee. So the empress gave a different imperial order instead, declaring that the peony be exiled from the capital. It was nothing but political symbolism, and people saw no point in openly confronting the empress.

The flower girl did not understand all that, but Xuanji should have known better. Such a poem could have been interpreted as a 'thought crime.'

'So you have the poem with you?'

'I think so, but it may take a while for me to find it,' she said, blushing again. 'My room is such a mess.'

'I'm staying at Dingguo Temple. I'll be there for a couple of days more. Can you send it to me when you get hold of it? Perhaps you may also bring some flowers for the temple.'

He fumbled in his inner pocket again.

'Don't worry about it, sir. The silver ingot you gave me more than covers that as well. But what were we talking about before shifting to the topic of the peony?'

'She came to your flower garden the day before the discovery of the maid's body in the nunnery backyard, right?'

'Yes, she came that morning, the second day of the month. She must have done some other shopping on the way to my flower garden.'

'For a special guest?'

'I would think so. In her basket, I noticed a tiny package of swallow saliva nest. A slice of dried shark fin. And some high-quality rice paper along with a fox-tail brush pen.'

'All so fancy and pricy!'

'Usually, the shopping was a job for her maid named Ning, but it's probably because of the expensive stuff that Xuanji did not trust her with it on this occasion. But I could not help feeling curious about such a shopping spree.'

'Did she say anything about the maid?'

'No, she did not. She was picking up the flowers with the shopping basket placed on the ground, and I took another look into the basket.'

'What else did you see?'

'She had a live bass, shrimp, and some fresh bean sprout. Not large quantities, not enough for a party, but more likely for one guest. A small bunch of fresh lychee. Oh, and an urn of Maiden Red, too.'

'Maiden Red?'

'It's a convention among some well-to-do people to bury an urn of Shaoxing rice wine in the ground on the birth of a daughter in the family. When she grows up, the people will dig the urn out on her wedding day – the wine is almost scarlet in color after it has been kept underground all these years. That's the origin of the name. But people don't have to drink it only on that special occasion. It's also an indication of the age of the wine, at least fifteen or sixteen years old, so mellow and smooth, and of course very expensive, too.'

Was there something else in the flower girl's sensual description of the special shopping Xuanji did for that day?

'Yes, not just with a high price tag, but with a very evocative name as well,' Judge Dee said, nodding. 'So the Maiden Red as well as other special items would have been prepared for a special guest in the intimacy of the intoxicating spring night, I would like to imagine.'

'I have no idea about the identity of the special visitor to her that night. At least, she did not mention anything about it to me. It's a bit unusual. She used to keep nothing from me, bragging and boasting about those big-bug visitors of hers. But for the last one or two months, she appeared to be mysterious – inexplicably mysterious. For one thing, she did not talk to me at all about that special guest, and she actually made a point of coming to my place for the flowers instead of having me deliver them to the nunnery.'

'That's something, I see. Anything else?'

'At times, she looked so radiant, as if with happiness pouring out from within, but the next moment, she could appear to be very pensive. It was just not like her.'

'In addition to unusual things about her, did you notice anything out of the ordinary at the nunnery?'

'No, I didn't – but now you mention it, there might have been something a little bit strange. The last time I went there

– it was more than half a month ago – I saw somebody – a man I had never seen before – standing outside the nunnery like a guard, who tried to bar me from entering. Then Xuanji herself hurried out, but she did not let me in, either. That's so weird. I have seen men staying inside the nunnery before – in her bedroom, too. That's no big deal – not something secret between us.'

'She used to keep nothing from you, I believe.'

'So the man she had been seeing that day must be somebody, as in an old proverb, "a divine dragon soaring in the cloud, with its head visible, but not with its tail."'

'*A divine dragon soaring in the cloud, with its head visible, but not with its tail*,' he echoed, shocked by so many coincidences of dragons in the last few days. Was that why his nerves had been so frayed with the mysterious case? 'Well, I've never heard of the proverb before.'

But it came to his realization that it was not a proverb, but more likely a quote in classical poetry criticism. Who had initially said it, however, he failed to recollect.

'I think that's what she once said to me about the guest. But sorry, my memories may be getting confused.'

'A different question, Zhang.' He could not help staring at her before he went on, abruptly changing the subject. 'How was the relationship between Xuanji and her maid Ning?'

'When she first moved into the nunnery, she brought Ning from her family as a little maidservant. In a couple of years, Ning turned out to be a clever, pretty, but rather coquettish young girl. Xuanji once complained to me about it. But with all those visitors of hers, a capable maidservant like Ning was not without some benefit.'

'I see,' he said, vaguely disturbed by the flower girl's description of Ning being *pretty but rather coquettish*. 'Just one more question for you. Did some of the visitors hit on the maidservant in addition to Xuanji?'

'That I don't know, but I don't think so. Xuanji is truly a great beauty. The fame of a celebrated poetess like Xuanji surely made a world of difference to the visitors. For a slip of an ordinary village girl like Ning, they had no need to come to the nunnery.'

'That's a good point. Thank you so much, Zhang. You have helped me a lot for the project of her poetry collection. The readers will be grateful to you, too.'

'Thank you, sir. I hope you will succeed with your endeavor. Here is just something small for you,' she said, handing him a tiny ball of white jasmine bud, which people could put in their hair or in a buttonhole.

But for an old bookish man like him?

Long after the solitary figure of Judge Dee vanished from the hill trail, Yang remained standing still in front of the temple, unable to shake off the feeling that his master might not have told him everything about the investigation.

Was it because there was too much risk involved in the investigation that Dee decided to prevent him from moving any further in that direction?

From the very beginning, Judge Dee had tried to downplay the seriousness of the ominous flying-knife note left in the hostel room, Yang contemplated.

In spite of Judge Dee's effort, what information he gathered the previous day convinced Yang, however, that things were far more complicated and sinister than a tall tale of a bewitching black fox spirit prowling around the nunnery.

There was hardly anything for Yang to do in the temple. The breakfast tasted so bland, with nothing but a small dish of soft tofu mixed with green onion and sesame oil, and a bowl of wishy-washy white rice porridge. Supposedly, a fashionable, delicious vegetarian treat to those men of letters, but not to him.

And the continuous mumbled chanting of the Buddhist scriptures in the service hall of the temple repeatedly reminded him of the green-headed flies buzzing and murmuring in Xuanji's backyard. It also brought along a suggestion of the onset of a dull headache.

The young monk Nameless came over to chat with him amiably, given that Judge Dee was not in the temple. Nameless and Yang failed, however, to find any common topic interesting to them both.

Shortly afterward, Yang sneaked out, too, wearing a smooth,

shiny bamboo hat made by an old monk squatting in the front yard of the temple, slicing the bamboo deftly with a long knife, and looking up with a toothless grin at Yang.

The sound of the bell wafting over in a fresh breeze outside the temple seemed to clear his head. Yang wondered whether Judge Dee was really taking a stroll around the temple in the hills. The day before, Yang recalled, Judge Dee had been listening to his report in earnest, raising a number of questions, and making some notes on a scrap of paper.

So was Judge Dee now checking with those possible clues and contacts by himself?

Halfway down the hill, Yang made an abrupt turn, heading toward the nunnery. It was only a little more than a mile from the temple. The distance was nothing to him.

With no one in the nunnery, Judge Dee would more likely be talking to people in the neighborhood, whose names and addresses he had learned from Yang. So it might be as well for the 'investigation assistant' to take a look into the nunnery instead, even though it was cordoned off.

There was one puzzle particularly inexplicable to Yang. The more inexplicable, the more he thought about it, while trudging through the surrounding stillness of the hills.

Several villagers had confirmed witnessing the black fox spirit stalking the neighborhood of the nunnery. Testimony from one villager could have been a matter of superstitious hallucination, but when it came from several of them, it appeared to be way beyond Yang, the more so with the movement of the fox spirit reportedly intensifying during the last couple of months. Could that have been an omen that something horrible was going to happen there?

Another sharp, unexpected turn of the trail brought Yang in view of the nunnery, which was closer than he had thought. Located almost at the foot of the hill, it remained cordoned off with yellow banners. The lawn in front of the nunnery was uncut, untrimmed for days, and the rampant wild weeds looked desolate in the morning light.

The nunnery was a one-story square building, with a strip of lawn in front, and a fairly large backyard. The yellowish painted walls were decked with intricate Daoist signs of yin and yang embossed in white and black. The front door was shut tight, presenting a shining brass padlock and an official seal issued by the mayor's office.

It might not be a good idea for him to try breaking into the nunnery at the present moment, given Judge Dee's sensitive situation. Still, he could not shake off a hunch that something might have been left undiscovered inside the nunnery. He decided to do some espionage work outside first.

Walking around the slightly discolored nunnery walls, he saw a small half-hidden trail stretching out from the back, the rampant weeds recently trodden here and there, leading to a shabby-looking wooden hut a short distance away. It could turn out to be Wei's.

The nunnery was not exactly a building standing in isolation. It was not a part of the village at the foot of the hill either, but just about a stone's throw away.

Yang moved down. It took him little effort to obtain from the villagers confirmation that the hut in question was indeed none other than Wei's.

A middle-aged villager with a long white-streaked beard claimed that he had seen a young woman like Xuanji trotting out barefoot and barelegged toward the hut on a summer night, her long black hair streaming like torrents in the breeze, but given the distance, he could not be too sure about it. An elderly gray-haired woman insisted she saw Wei heading toward the nunnery in raven-black clothing one dark night, like a stealthy animal.

'Like a black fox spirit? No, she's the black fox spirit. I tell you! What a shameless bitch! A black curse on the whole neighborhood.'

So Wei and Xuanji must have been seeing each other under the cover of darkness. That's probably why she had purchased for him the shelter nearby. But how could she have still been that crazy about him?

Incidentally, their nocturnal rendezvous could also have given rise to those more vivid, more absurd stories about the black fox spirit with the indistinct, suspicious figures skulking back and forth in the depth of the night.

'Last night my neighbor saw a black animal scurrying

toward the nunnery like crazy, with a long tail trailing along the ground, and two ghastly green eyes glaring daggers in the dark.'

A new idea hit Yang. 'Last night' was after Xuanji had been thrown into prison. But Wei still remained at large out there. So Wei could have sneaked in and out of the nunnery for the valuable stuff left inside it. An 'insatiable leech,' as Yang had heard Wei described the previous day.

Yang went on talking to the people in the village. Having learned the lesson the day before, he was focusing on Wei instead, with the same excuse of trying to get antiques – except now through Wei – from the nunnery.

'You have come to the very man for information,' a middle-aged villager nicknamed Big Head Zhao declared with a loud chuckle. 'He sold me a pair of solid silver candle stands just two or three days ago.'

'Wow, solid silver candle stands. Quite valuable.'

'Not his own, you bet. He could hardly afford to burn a candle at night.'

'So he stole them from somewhere?'

'From the nunnery, you bet again. He has a key to the backdoor – he once boasted and bragged about it to me – so he may not call it stealing.'

'Whatever he wants to call it, do you think I can have a talk with him? He may still have some other expensive knick-knacks left behind for me.'

'Not right now, I'm afraid. An impossible night animal, he usually sleeps until midday before going out to the city, where he hangs around at one place or another, drinking or partying until past midnight. Afterward, Old Heaven alone knows what he would be up to with that damned bitch waiting naked for him in the nunnery, moaning and groaning in bed.'

'Night animals indeed,' Yang said echoing. 'Has there been anything unusual about him of late?'

'He's been worried, crest-fallen the moment she was thrown into prison. He's already been to the pawnshop several times, carrying big or small bags. She won't be coming out of prison, he knows. Whatever may be left inside the nunnery, he has to turn it into cash as quickly as possible.' Big Head Zhao added after a dramatic pause, 'And he sold some of the cheap furniture, too – from his own hut.'

That would probably not be worth much. The cheap furniture in the shabby hut. Yang could not help wondering how Wei would have been that desperate.

Unless Wei was about to flee?

In that case, it could have pointed to a possible connection not yet known between Wei and Xuanji in the murder case.

Yang then moved back to the nunnery, circling the yellow walls against the green weeping willows.

This time he came to notice something else. The soil near that spot in the backyard turned out to be very hard, as he was able to tell by stamping his foot forcibly on it. He did not have to use a spade to test it.

It would have been far from easy for a delicate woman like Xuanji to dig out, single-handedly, the space large and deep enough for a body to be buried properly in it. Not easy even for such a sloppy job as barely covered the maid's body under a thin surface of soil.

Besides, what with expected and unexpected visitors frequently dropping in and out of the nunnery, and with the village people passing around from time to time, there was no possibility of her doing the burial job in the backyard during the day. It had to be done at night, and even then in a quick and quiet way – no lanterns raised, no noise made.

None of her neighbors had seen or heard her moving, working there that night. Nor did the night watchman patrolling around four or five times during the night notice anything unusual and submit a report about it.

In short, Xuanji did not have the strength for a quick and quiet burial job without being noticed. It was not a job she could have done there by herself.

According to the villagers, everything was possible, of course, in the scenario of the supernatural black fox spirit; like his master, however, Yang did not believe in it.

He managed to circle the nunnery a couple of more times, still unable to get hold of anything like a possible clue, or to get rid of the vague premonition that somebody else might have been prowling around behind his back.

Outside the flower garden, Judge Dee sniffed at the jasmine bud once again, shaking his head with a touch of self-satire before sticking it in the buttonhole of his blue cloth gown.

'Just a sentimental old fool,' he said to himself, trying to ridicule himself out of the gloom, 'wandering spellbound in the midst of flowers.'

He was going to follow what he had learned from the flower girl – to the shops and stores in accordance with Xuanji's shopping list of the day: the farmer's market for the fish and shrimp, the herbal store for the swallow saliva nest and dried shark fin, the tavern for the Shaoxing rice wine called 'Maiden Red,' and the stationery shop for purple skunk- or fox-tail brush pen.

To his relief, the authorization note from Minister Wu proved to be truly helpful to his inquiries at those places. The note did not reveal his identity, but the red official seal was more than enough for people to respond readily to his questions.

In the event of his movement being reported to the high authorities, he thought that it was such an irony as would work in his favor. The report could actually serve as another confirmation that the conscientious, honest Judge Dee had looked closely into the case.

According to the people he approached, what Xuanji bought on that day – the second day of the month – was confirmed to be extraordinarily expensive, yet all in tiny quantities. That corroborated what he had gathered from the flower girl. The shopping Xuanji did that day was just for one special guest, though there appeared to be some unexpectedly intriguing details from those shops.

At the stationery store, the owner named Xiahou told Judge Dee that the purple skunk-tail brush pen had been custom-ordered by her along with a roll of green bamboo paper, and that she had mentioned she was going to write for someone special, so Xiahou did not have to worry about the cost. In the herbal store, Judge Dee was told that having bargained hard with the sales assistant, Xuanji ended up purchasing only the minimum amount of swallow saliva nest of the highest quality instead of a whole box, saying she was going to make the drink for just one guest.

But these details did not necessarily contradict her earlier statements. It was still possible that instead of preparing for a visitor that evening, she could have chosen the delicacies for her own indulgence. Indeed, swallow saliva nest was said to be capable of making a woman's face look young and radiant.

But the scenario did not add up. Judge Dee began sweating again, mopping his brow, feeling tired and drowsy as he dragged his heavy feet out of the last store on the shopping list and into the sunlight.

What would a woman like Xuanji have done after such a shopping spree?

Back in the nunnery, probably a nap first. Afterward, she would be able to meet her guest, appearing fresh and energetic.

Alternatively, she would have started preparing for the lavish dinner in the evening. Gourmets made a point of having the live fish and shrimp prepared immediately from the food market; otherwise, the river food would lose much of its fresh flavor. The more so for a gastronomic treat – whether for herself or an unusual guest.

How, then, could she have left the food unprepared and started drinking by herself like crazy?

Judge Dee too felt very thirsty all of a sudden.

It would be good to have a cup of rice wine at a street-corner tavern, but he plodded on, thinking like a puppet controlled by an invisible string.

With those questions unanswered in his mind, Judge Dee decided he had to make a visit to the typesetter/publisher surnamed Mo.

Judging from the information he had gleaned from Xiahou at the stationery store, the unknown guest for whom Xuanji had done the exceptional shopping appeared to be a man truly appreciative of her poetry. As diligent an investigative assistant as Yang might have been, he knew too little about the literary jargon mouthed by Mo.

Unsurprisingly, Mo turned out to be a bookish Li loyalist, which was why he had readily given Yang his cherished proof with Xuanji's changes and comments on it. Presumably a Confucianist, too, capable of thinking only in the logics of the orthodox Confucian doctrines, Mo had taken Judge Dee as just another Li loyalist like himself.

'As in an ancient proverb, a sturdy pine tree proves itself standing firm, unbreakable against the storm. We've heard of your wise advice to the empress about the rightful succession of the Li family. And you have landed yourself into trouble because of your allegiance to the Li family. It's right and proper, however, for all of us to follow the time-honored tradition of Confucianism, though I'm nothing compared with you. So anything I can possibly do to help, Your Honor, you just name it.'

'Thank you so much, Mr Mo. You may go ahead and tell me what you know about Xuanji and her work – and the people she's associated with.'

'Where shall I begin, Your Honor? I hardly knew anything about Xuanji until she moved into the nunnery.'

'To start with, you may tell me anything that struck you as unusual about her of late. Particularly over the last couple of months.'

'Yesterday, your assistant Yang and I talked about the collection of her poems. Afterward, I searched for the poems she had left with me – she did not give me all of her poems in one sitting – but I found one piece not included in the previous collection. It's titled "Letter to Wen Tingyun on a Winter Night":

> *'Thinking hard, I search for the lines*
> *to recite under the lamplight,*
> *too nervous to spend the sleepless,*
> *long night under the chilly quilt,*
> *with the leaves trembling, falling*
> *in the courtyard, fearful*
> *of the wind coming,*

and the curtain flapping
forlornly under the moon sinking . . .

Busy or not, I am always aware
of the unquenchable yearning
deep inside me. My heart remains
unchanged through the ups and downs.
The parasol tree being no place
for perching, a lone bird circles
the woods at dusk, chirping,
and chirping in vain.'

'You see, that's in her characteristic style, full of lyrical intensity, yet restrained.'

'Yes, the metaphor about the lone bird circling and chirping in vain for a place to perch really speaks for herself,' Judge Dee said, nodding in appreciation. 'The combination of "chilly quilt," "the leaves trembling, falling," and "the parasol tree" makes an exquisite poem.'

'But now you mention it, Your Honor, there's something unusual she wanted me to do of late – in addition to that published edition. About a month ago, Xuanji talked to me about another possible project of new poems for an extremely limited edition – with no more than two copies in total. It's strange. The woodblock engraving would be charged by the number of engraved wooden blocks, as you know. It does not make sense to print only two copies. For two copies, why not have handwritten copies done by a well-known calligrapher? Far less expensive, and far more valuable as a collectible. But she insisted on the printed copies, and on the best-quality paper, too.'

'That's very unusual.'

'And that collection contains only seven or eight poems in all. She showed one of the poems to me. A very passionate piece, almost too explicit for my taste, and not restrained like her other poems. She could have composed it for a new lover.'

'Do you have a copy of the poem, Mr Mo?'

'She took it back, I think, but I can double-check for you. At the time, she discussed with me some details. She said she would bring over the complete manuscript soon. And she was emphatic that she would not spare the cost. The best-quality paper and printing.'

'Could she have written it for Wen or Zi'an? Love poems of the intimate moments in their company?'

'No, Wen was seriously ill at home in Hebei Province. Zi'an was also far away in another province, too busy with his official responsibilities, and with his jealous wife watching him ever so closely.' Mo added with a frown, 'It's not merely that it was in a different style from those she wrote for Wen or Zi'an. The contents—'

'What about the contents?'

'It's full of gratitude for the nourishment of the rain and dew she receives from the man.'

'Sort of erotic?'

'You can say that again. Considering the fact that Wen pushed her to Zi'an, and Zi'an hurt her badly by his desertion, I cannot imagine her writing a sentimentally gushing poem like that – like a woman falling head over heels in love.'

'That's true, but how about the scenario of her writing these poems for Wei?'

'You know about Wei, too! Yes, she lost her head over him for a while, but that was about a year ago. Soon she ceased to take him seriously anymore. For a sexually strong woman like her, however, it might not be enough for her to live in the world of poems, and in the meantime, Wei continued to appeal to her as an unrivaled bed companion. As for that limited edition of those graphic love poems, she would never have had Wei in mind, who hardly understood those lines.'

'That's a very perceptive point. I would say you're right again, Mr Mo. Do you think that the limited edition was to be done for someone who recently came to her poetry parties in the nunnery?'

'That's quite possible. She talked with her guests about poetry over tea or wine in the evening. Poetry served, more often than not, just as an excuse, for them. From time to time, after a fancy dinner, a special guest with some extraordinary gift or an extra-thick red envelope could choose to spend the night there – supposedly in another room of the nunnery.'

'A special guest indeed.'

'Among those guests, Xuanji had a special one named Jinren, a prosperous silk merchant. An obscenely rich man, he practically covered a large part of the daily expenses for the nunnery, in return for which she had a poem dedicated to him. While an acknowledged patron, he did not mind her seeing other men. A different duck indeed.'

'She has certainly had a colorful life. Do you think Jinren could have been the one that inspired the poem in the latest edition she proposed to you?'

'No, I don't think so. Jinren is a fan of her fame and beauty, but not of her poems. In terms of social status, Jinren is not even on a par with Wen or Zi'an. Besides, in that poem she showed to me, she compares her man of extraordinarily high social status to a dragon soaring high in the white clouds.'

'A soaring dragon!' Dee exclaimed, the tea rippling out of the cup in his hand. 'So high!'

At the exit of the village, Yang looked over his shoulder, taking one more glance back at the nunnery, which appeared to be like a silhouette of an animal crouching against the hills, yet ready to jump up at him at any moment.

Spitting on the ground, he thought he might have been hearing too much of those blood-curdling black fox spirit tales for the last couple of days.

It was understandable that village people chose not to come close to the nunnery. With Xuanji gone, it could eventually turn into a den for real foxes.

Once again, Yang found himself heading back toward that shoddy wooden hut of Wei's. It was past noon-time. Wei should be up by now. Though hardly a suspect at the present moment, Wei was likely a man capable of telling Yang something more – something more intimate – about Xuanji.

As Yang was sidling toward the hut, its door flung open with a bang. Still at a distance, he thought he had heard a clanging sound inside the hut, like some heavy furniture being overturned on to the ground.

Yang jumped off the trail and, taking several steps in haste, hid himself behind an apple tree blossoming transparently white in the noon light.

Sure enough, he caught sight of Wei dashing out of the hut and hurrying straight to the nunnery. It might be a good opportunity for him to follow Wei, so he could find out more about things between Wei and Xuanji, an opening Yang could not afford to miss.

He sneaked out from behind the blossoming apple tree and shadowed Wei at a cautious distance. In front of him, Wei started trotting in agitation, carrying a gray cloth bundle on his back, and stumbling along the trail through the tall weeds.

With Wei vanishing through the back door of the nunnery, Yang came to an abrupt stop.

Wei appeared to be ready to flee with the gray bundle containing the valuable stuff from the hut. So his sneaky visit to the nunnery could have been made for the same purpose. Yang decided that he might as well wait outside. There could be something valuable for him to take from the nunnery, too. Squatting behind a large white-streaked black rock, he kept wiping the sweat rivulets off his brows with the back of his hand.

Something stirred surreptitiously, all of a sudden, in the surrounding weeds, which startled Yang. It turned out to be an enormous brown rabbit, shooting away like an arrow. Yang wondered whether small animals like that could have appeared as the black fox spirit in those villagers' imagination.

It did not take too long for Yang to see Wei emerging from the nunnery, carrying the same gray cloth bundle, which now seemed to be much larger. Something more could have been stuffed in the bundle that Wei ransacked from the nunnery.

Instead of turning back to the hut, Wei headed down toward the road that stretched out in front of the nunnery. It led to the town, Yang observed. The scenario of Wei's fleeing with things in the bundle appeared to be even more likely.

It was then up to Yang to resume shadowing the fugitive.

Moving toward the open road at the foot of the hill, Yang was compelled to pursue him more discreetly. He had to keep a greater distance between them. There appeared to be fewer trees and less overgrowth to act as cover along the roadsides.

He began debating with himself as to whether he should put on a spurt and stop Wei then and there for questioning.

It was then he heard a horse neighing, as if out of the blue, from behind a bend in the road. Hastening back several steps into a narrower trail to one side, he looked up at the sight of a black-attired-and-hooded man spurring his black horse in Wei's direction.

Yang stood still, staring at the scene like one under a spell before it occurred to him that the black horseman had been chasing, closing in, whipping at the horse furiously, and crashing toward Wei at full speed.

Confounded, Yang stumbled as he tried to rush out in Wei's direction. His arms flailing in the air, he fell with a heavy thud before he got out of his hiding place. The sharp pain of a badly sprained ankle took his breath away.

As he managed to get up with a fast-swelling ankle and limped out into the open, both the horseman and Wei seemed to have vanished into thin air. There was no trace whatsoever left visible on the road.

It was none too surprising as far as the mysterious rider in black was concerned, but how could Wei also have disappeared so quickly?

Yang's glance kept sweeping around. Then it came to rest on some red spots like bloodstains which led to a tree-shaded side of the road. There he spotted a figure lying grotesquely in something like a dried ditch, partially buried under damp, dirty weeds.

Hurrying over, he was struck with the recognition that it was Wei's body lying there in a twisted heap, with small pools of blood congealing around his head and body.

Yang leaned down, reaching out to touch the fallen one's neck gingerly. There was no pulse that he could find. The body was starting to get cold.

Wei had been killed. He had two vicious slashes at the head and shoulder – possibly the fatal ones delivered with a sword or a saber from above – and a third wound, a deep stab inflicted at the groin.

It was evident that Wei had been ambushed there.

Then something missing from the scene grabbed Yang's

attention. The gray cloth bundle had disappeared. The black-attired-and-hooded horseman must have ridden away with it.

Could that have been the very reason for the fatal ambush?

For a poor-as-a-rat, good-for-nothing man like Wei, however, it seemed to be hardly conceivable.

Unless there was something really valuable in the gray cloth bundle. But could it be so valuable – whether out of Wei's hut or Xuanji's nunnery – as to make him a robbery target in broad daylight?

For the ambush, the horseman had to have been staying somewhere nearby, and for quite a long period of time until Wei stepped out of the nunnery and moved down to the road. And it was only then that the killer could have galloped over at full speed.

And for the ambush, it was not just a matter of long, long waiting with no certainty. The scene of a black-attired-and-hooded rider on his black horse tarrying about the small village would have been suspicious enough to attract the attention of the people there. Was it worth the risk?

Besides, how could the perpetrator have possibly known for sure that Wei would come out of the nunnery with that gray bundle on his back, and move down to that particular section of the road?

Frowning, Yang hastened to bend down to re-examine the body. Soon the local people would be rushing out to the crime scene. He had to do his job before their arrival.

His re-examination alerted him to something else. The first slash aimed at Wei's head, delivered from above, was such a forceful one that it must have finished Wei instantly. The second stroke was probably dispatched for the sake of insurance. It was impossible, however, to reconstruct the scene of the thrust at the groin from the attacker on the horseback; he had to have dismounted for that stab.

Why should he have taken all that trouble to do so?

Unless he wanted to make a deliberate statement with the particular locality of the wound.

With Wei being a notorious womanizer, the message could have pointed to the price he had to pay for taking the liberty of touching an untouchable woman.

But Wei was known to have been 'kept' by Xuanji. Could it have possibly been Xuanji?

He bent over the body for a last look at the crime scene in haste.

It was in the late afternoon that Judge Dee got back to his room in the temple, with a weariness weighing down on him like a heavy rock. Pulling his swollen feet out of his boots, he changed into a pair of straw slippers provided by the temple, and heaved a sigh of relief.

He made himself a cup of lukewarm tea, took the jasmine bud out of the buttonhole of his gown, put it into the tea, inhaled the light fragrance spreading in the cup, and pulled the armchair closer to the open window.

In the distance, a solitary wild goose appeared to be flying over a discolored pavilion on the distant hillside, its wings flapping against the oppressive sky. Resting his elbow on the arm of his chair, and his chin on his fist, he stared at the desolate scene in the approaching gloom, trying to sort through what he had learned earlier in the day.

With his and Yang's information put together, however, he failed to produce anything close to a scenario plausible even to himself.

As he had discussed with Han Shan the previous day, he was unable to put his finger on Xuanji's motive for killing the maidservant.

Nor for such a deadly plot against Xuanji.

But he could only afford to stay on the outskirts of Chang'an for a couple more days.

The way the investigation was going, it would probably take much longer for him to achieve a breakthrough. In the meantime, there was a disturbing premonition that loomed in the darksome background of the case, involving a much higher, more sinister political stake way beyond his grasp.

It was necessary, consequently, for him to find another way to carry out the investigation. In other words, Judge Dee had no choice but to step out into the open.

He started grinding the mountain-pine-smoke inkstick slowly on a Duan ink stone, circle by circle, before he picked up a new brush pen. Moistening the starched brush tip on his tongue, he dipped it into the ink, and put down a list of puzzling questions on a piece of paper.

After gazing at the list of questions for a long while, he twirled the pen and drew a line in a tentative connection between two of them.

For whom had she done the extraordinary shopping, sparing no expense, in preparation for the special dinner that evening?

For whom had she planned to produce the limited poetry edition – with a print of only two copies in all?

Studying them intently, he commented in bold strokes in the margin between the two lines in a response to himself:

For someone special.

It had to be someone far more special than either Wen or Zi'an – at least at the present moment of her life.

Even in the event of 'someone special' being identified, however, Judge Dee still failed to grasp a convincing connection with the bizarre murder case.

Again, his reverie was interrupted by a knock on the door, which was pushed open before Judge Dee turned around.

It was Yang striding into the room in heavy steps and closing the door behind him in a hurry.

'Where have you been, Yang? Nameless told me that you also left the temple in the morning.'

'I'm not a man for the leisure of the temple – you know me, Master. So I, too, took a walk – around the village, the hut, and the nunnery.'

Yang's response came as no surprise to Judge Dee, who had anticipated such a move on the part of his ever-energetic, self-styled 'assistant in investigation.'

'Wei's hut, you mean?'

Instead of responding to Judge Dee's question, Yang put on the table something that more than astonished his master. In spite of himself, Judge Dee took in a deep, sharp breath at the object lying on the table.

A blood-stained yellow silk underrobe.

'Where did you get it, Yang?'

'It was wrapped around Wei's waist like a sort of money

belt with the two sleeves tied in a knot at the front, except that it was wrapped inside his long gown.'

'What! From Wei's waist?'

'Wei was attacked by a horseman on the road in front of the nunnery – shortly after he sneaked out of it in the afternoon, carrying a large gray cloth bundle on his back. I rushed over to the scene, but Wei was already dead and the bundle gone.'

Leaning over for a closer look at the rumpled yellow underrobe, Judge Dee was shocked by the color as well as the details of the embossed dragon pattern on the extraordinary clothing.

It was a man's underrobe. So its presence in Xuanji's nunnery suggested that it had been either given to her as a token of intimacy, or left there as the man had to wear it from time to time in her company at night. In other words, it had belonged to a regular, intimate visitor to her bedroom. Neither possibility turned out to be, however, a scenario shockingly unbelievable to the experienced Judge Dee.

For the moment, he did not think it was wise for him to discuss with Yang the staggering new scenario that was forming in his mind.

'Tell me more about it, Yang. Tell me from the very beginning of the research you have done today. It may be of paramount importance to the murder investigation.'

Yang started narrating about what he had seen, heard, and done during the day before he shifted to focus on the fatal ambush in the neighborhood of the nunnery. Pausing to take a sip of the cold tea, he raised a question with a deep-knitted frown cut across his forehead.

'I examined Wei's body closely. There's something I don't understand, Master. The two slashes at the head and shoulder were inflicted with a sword-like weapon from above. That made sense from the attacker on horseback.'

'What, then, did not make sense?'

'The vicious thrust at the groin. Why? The attacker had to dismount to do so.'

'You have a good point. It was done, I would guess, for the sake of leaving a specific message.'

'That's what I thought, too. A message saying that the killing was a punishment for his relationship with a woman he should not have touched. In other words, it indicates the reason why Wei has been killed.'

'Yes?'

'But in relation to a woman like Xuanji – a notorious, promiscuous courtesan – it does not make any sense. After all, what she did after those poetry parties with those guests in the nunnery was no secret.'

'So there must be something else beyond our knowledge about the case. Now, you've just mentioned that the attacker got away with the gray cloth bundle Wei had carried on his back – was there anything suspicious about the bundle?'

'Yes, but could whatever was in the bundle have been enough for the ambushing and killing in broad daylight?'

'Probably not in terms of its material value, but for something else it was definitely worth it. At least, so it must have seemed to the attacker. Or to the one who gave the order to the attacker from above. And that's what we have to find out.'

'So Wei became aware of the approaching danger that was known only to him, tried to flee with the bundle, but he did not make it in the end?'

'There're a lot of things inscrutable to us,' Judge Dee said, adding hot water to Yang's cup. 'In fact, I've been to her neighborhood, too, but I've learned far less. So I think I need to do some more thinking about the case in the light of your latest discovery. For one thing, I'm wondering whether the two murders could be related. The murder in the backyard of the nunnery, and the murder on the road in the neighborhood of the nunnery.'

'The two murders related?'

'I'm just wondering about the possibility.' Then Judge Dee changed the subject abruptly, tapping at the table with his fingertip. 'Do you think Wei came out of Xuanji's place with that yellow silk underrobe?'

'I'm not sure whether he had it from his own hut or from the nunnery. It was wrapped inside his gown, but I do not think it likely that he had the yellow underrobe with him when he stepped out of the hut.'

'Tell me why?'

'If it's in the hut, he would have put it in the bundle. On the other hand, he could have ferreted it out at the last minute in the nunnery with the bundle already packed and knotted. Too much trouble for him to undo it. That's why he wrapped the underrobe around his waist. Perhaps something of potential value in his mind – high-quality silk with exquisite embroidery – so he wrapped it around his waist as quickly as possible.'

'I think you're right, Yang.'

'Then, after he fell, and I lifted his gown to check the wound in his groin, I caught sight of the yellow underrobe for the first time. Its color was quite eye-catching out there in the sunlight.'

'Now, here's a curious question for you. What prompted you to bring the underrobe to me, Yang?'

'I don't know exactly, Master. It just seemed so odd to me. People may occasionally wear their clothing that way when it's getting too warm outside. It's for convenience's sake. But in Wei's case, it was wrapped inside his gown.'

'Wrapped around the waist inside the gown?'

'Yes, like a sort of belt bag. For silver or gold or something extraordinarily valuable, some people may choose to wear a belt bag concealed like that. Against the possibility of pick-pocketing, you know. But I double-checked there, and there's nothing very valuable within the underrobe. Not even a single pocket. So I took it from Wei's body.'

'So it could be something of potential value. Or something of sentimental value – the underrobe he wore in her bedroom, in her company,' Judge Dee said reflectively, caressing the fabric again. 'It's made of real silk. Premium quality. I don't think Wei could have afforded it.'

'Yes, it's made of high-quality silk, and embroidered with dragons in gold threads, too. I don't think I have ever seen such an exquisite one.'

'The color, the design, the material – all really unusual—' Judge Dee said, making a hasty decision not to go any further for the moment. 'Well, we may have to do something different tomorrow, I think.'

'What do you mean, Master?'

'Let's go to visit Mayor Pei.'

'Yes, Mayor Pei must have been so worried about the murder case. The local folk are becoming increasingly paranoid of the evil cast by the black fox spirit – already two deaths, and another one soon with the execution of Xuanji, all of them seemingly interconnected in one way or another. Several nervous folk are said to be ready to flee the village, which appears to be haunted in their mind.'

'Yes, that may serve as a very convenient pretext for the discussion of the murder case with Mayor Pei. I have met him a few times before. A very capable official. We'll have a lot to discuss about the complicated case. Any possible aspect or angle is worth exploring.'

'But you're leaving for that new post of yours, Master. At the end of the day, it's not your case. Whether you may be able to do anything by stepping out into the open, no one could tell. With only one or two days more for your stay here, what difference can you possibly make?'

'*Knowing it's something impossible for you to do, you still have to try your best at it, as long as it is right and proper for you to do so*,' Judge Dee said. 'That's a Confucian maxim my late father used to quote for me. At least I should have a try.'

There was no point alarming Yang with these new scenarios flashing through his mind. And Judge Dee was still wondering what could prove to be the 'right and proper' thing for him to do when a light knock came at the door.

It was the young monk Nameless standing in the doorway, scratching his shaved head, and holding an envelope in his hand with a mysterious air.

'A flower girl in the neighborhood has just delivered the letter here, saying it's something Your Honor may be interested in reading.'

'Oh, the flower girl Zhang,' Judge Dee said, taking the envelope from Nameless. 'I bought some flowers from her earlier in the day. Let her come in.'

'No, she has left. Conventionally, a female visitor like the flower girl would be barred from entering here unless for some religious service arranged beforehand. So she gave the letter to me without coming in.'

'I see. Coincidentally, I had intended to have a special service arranged here for my late parents. Your temple is well known, but I may not have the time for it right now, I'm afraid. I'm going to leave for the new post in a day or two,' Judge Dee said, taking a piece of paper from the envelope.

'Yes, Master has discussed with me his plan for a religious service in the temple,' Yang said, chipping in, 'but Her Majesty insists on his leaving for the important new position without delay.'

'Oh, this is one of Xuanji's recent poems I have not read before,' Judge Dee said, glancing through the lines on the paper. 'She left it at the flower girl's. So intriguing. It may be very important for the compilation of her poetry collection.'

Alternatively, important for something more than the compilation of the poetry collection?

The question, however elusive, seemed to remain as he began to read the poem more closely.

'No wonder people choose to describe you as "infallible Judge Dee as clear as the cloudless sky,"' Nameless said with an ingratiating chuckle, 'even though your official rank is much higher, as Han Shan has told me. Just in one single day, you've interviewed so many people connected with Xuanji through your investigation.'

'Not so many, Nameless. And "judge" is but a convenient title for others, as I've served in so many different positions that I myself can hardly remember all the titles. What's more important, I'm not here for the investigation of the murder case.'

'But it's such an intriguing case as you have discussed with Han Shan.'

'As I have told you, I'm here for the project of compiling a new poetry collection of Xuanji. I'm taking a look into the case simply because it makes up a part of the much-needed backdrop for her poetry. On the other hand, it is Yang who has done a good job inquiring about those poems of Xuanji's so far unknown and uncollected. If that's the investigation you're talking about, it's really to Yang's credit. Because of his good work, I was able to approach the flower girl, for whom Xuanji wrote a couple of poems. And you see, here's one of the poems Xuanji dashed out in the flower garden.'

'It will surely be a successful project, Your Honor, that collection of Xuanji's poems. And Yang is a capable assistant for your worthy literary project, I totally agree,' Nameless said, changing the subject readily, nodding, and producing two candles out of his enormous sleeves. 'By the way, I'm bringing a pair of large candles for you. Pilgrims make a point of donating candles to the Buddha images in the temple. The weightier the candles, the more devout the pilgrims. These are two-catty ones. You can read as many poems as you like in the evening, but don't stay up too late, Your Honor.'

'Don't stay up too late again, Master,' Yang said aside, echoing as he turned to step out of the room, leaving in the company of Nameless.

Left alone in the room, Judge Dee was listening to the rain pattering against the window, picking up the cup of tea, when he became aware of a black bat flitting over the courtyard, hovering around, hissing portentously, as if anxious to break in through the white paper of the window. It appeared to be another ominous sign. Making an effort to laugh himself out of his apprehensive mood, he tried to assure himself that his nerves had been overwrought for the last couple of days.

So he turned to spread out on the table the paper with the poem on it. From time to time, poetry could soothe the tension, he knew from past experience. It was Xuanji's elegant handwriting, which he recognized at once.

'*The Fading Peony*.' He was murmuring to himself the title of the poem, stroking his gray beard, when he was thunderstruck by something in it.

It was too much of a political taboo for Xuanji to write about the topic of a peony under the reign of Empress Wu. The thought flashed through his mind. Even more so given Xuanji's singular treatment in those lines.

So much so, it could have served as an unquestionable evidence of the so-called thoughtcrime. Another characteristic of the Tang Empire. A word or a phrase, let alone a poem, interpreted as possibly against the interest of the supreme ruler could put the offender in prison. Xuanji should have known better than to make such a blunder.

Was it possible that she had composed the poem purposely for someone capable of appreciating it because of its political incorrectness?

Studying 'The Fading Peony' under the candlelight for the third or fourth time, he had a feeling that some of the dots accumulated at random during the last few days were beginning to scramble for connection in his mind – the knife note in the hostel, the signs from the *Book of Changes*, the unexpected request for help from the powerful Minister Wu, the intensified apparition of the black fox spirit in the neighborhood of the nunnery, the discussion with the publisher Mo about the unheard-of edition of only two copies, the murder of Wei in broad daylight, the yellow silk underrobe embroidered with dragons wrapped around his waist inside the gown, and Mayor Pei's complaining about somebody high above relentlessly pushing for the investigation to get to the very bottom . . .

But his train of thought was interrupted by loud, agitated knocks on the door.

Again it was Yang, who must have come running back, pushing open the door without waiting for Judge Dee to say 'Come in.'

'She's dead, Master.'

'Who are you talking about?'

'The flower girl surnamed Zhang. She's dead.'

'Wasn't she just at the temple a while ago, delivering that poem written by Xuanji?'

'Yes, that's her, but what the devil – two deaths in a single day,' Yang said, still speaking incoherently, as he moved over from the doorway. Taking another deep breath, he managed to regain some composure and started narrating about the second death he had just encountered 'in a single day.'

As it turned out, Yang could not help feeling curious about the flower girl's surprise visit to the temple, carrying Xuanji's poem, though he knew better than to discuss its implication in the company of Nameless when he delivered the letter from the flower girl.

After parting with Nameless, Yang walked out alone. It was quite dark outside the temple. There was no sign of the flower girl. Unfamiliar with the neighborhood, he had no idea about which direction she could have turned. The road appeared quite deserted. He remained standing under the night sky, looking left and right, with nothing but several will-o'-the-wisps floating eerily by the roadside.

His glance sweeping around the vicinity of the temple one more time, he was ready to head back when he heard a dog beginning to bark violently in the distance, even though it somehow seemed not to be too far away.

He lost no time turning in that direction. The barking remained audible, off and on, echoing into the somber sky as Yang fumbled along in the dark. The road soon forked into a shaded trail. And then the sound abruptly stopped.

It took him less than the time it took to burn incense to come striding into view of something lying on the turn of the trail, where rainwater seemed to be shimmering under the faint starlight. To his horror, it turned out to be the flower girl's body in pools of blood. Her clothing was badly torn, revealing her bare breasts and thighs. It appeared to be pointing to a sex crime, though she had been stabbed multiple times, as if the attacker had intended to kill.

One stab at her head, cutting deep into the right temple. Two more in her chest, with a forceful one close to the heart, leaving scarlet rivulets on the trail beside her. And the final one, viciously into her lower abdomen.

He put his right hand above her lips. He was unable to detect a breath in her. The blood smearing her face seemed to be still sticky to his finger. It had happened just a short while ago. Possibly at the moment the dog started barking.

He came to the realization that she was beyond help. There was no point dragging her body back to the temple, where the monks could do nothing about the dead flower girl. Besides, it was not a good idea to bring a female visitor to the temple, as he had just learned from Nameless – not to mention the possible scandal of moving a dead, half-naked girl into it.

After searching through the scene another time, Yang headed back to the temple, empty-handed.

It took quite a while for Yang to finish his account about the murder of the flower girl. Judge Dee made no interruption during Yang's narration. Then he said simply, 'Two victims in a day.'

'Yes, both of them related to Xuanji. But we have to leave in a day or two, Master.'

'But you have really done so much today. It's quite late, Yang. Time for you to go to bed. And I won't stay up for too long, either.'

With Yang's figure retreating out of the room, Judge Dee found himself overwhelmed in the entangling swirls of the old and new scenarios.

Indeed, it was quite late. He touched the buttonhole of his long gown, where he had inserted the jasmine bud earlier in the day. It was empty.

Judge Dee had to hold himself responsible – at least partially – for the flower girl's death, though no one could have foretold that her delivering the poem to the temple would have brought her young life to such a tragic end. In the final analysis, however, had he not paid the visit to her on the pretext of the poetry collection, she would not have come over to the temple at night – to her untimely end.

But in an increasingly probable scenario, like the murder of Wei, the murder of the flower girl appeared, more likely than not, to have been related to Xuanji's murder case.

If so, she had been forever silenced for the same reason as in Wei's case. For that matter, anyone close to Xuanji had to be eliminated lest they speak out about her relationship with the man in the yellow underrobe.

The one who had given the order for the killing of Wei, and then of the flower girl, must have been resourceful – maneuvering, planning, and waiting in the dark. Her visit to the temple at night had finally provided the opportunity they had been waiting for.

Instead of attacking her on the way to the temple, the attacker must have waited to find out first where she was going, but on her way back home, he struck out.

In that scenario, it would probably not take long for the people crouching in the dark to find out that Judge Dee was staying in the temple that night, the receiver of whatever information the flower girl had to deliver. The connection made, Judge Dee could be next on the killer's list . . .

He could not rule out the possibility, but it was more likely he had been panic-stricken like an arrow-wounded bird flustering at the furtive sound of a twang in the night woods.

With an abrupt sparkle, the large candle sputtered out, and he came to find himself lost in an overwhelming darkness.

FOUR

It took longer than expected for Judge Dee to reach Mayor Pei's official residence, but it was still early in the morning. He got down from the carriage, taking in a deep breath of the fresh air. Here and there, birds were heard twittering amid the fallen petals after a night of rain.

Mayor Pei came out in a hurry to meet them at the vermilion-painted gate.

'Sorry for the unannounced visit this morning, Mayor Pei,' Judge Dee said with a bow.

'It's such an honor for you to make the visit to my humble abode, Your Honor. Welcome. Please come in.'

Mayor Pei must have scrambled out for the surprise visit, wearing a sapphire-blue gown not yet properly buttoned up, and a black silk cap decorated with a green jade. He was a tall man with a neatly trimmed beard, which somehow added a touch of bookishness to his square face.

'Mayor Pei, this is my assistant, Yang. He is going to have the carriage horses fed outside. So don't worry about him. We'll have a good talk, just the two of us. Indeed, it's long time no see.'

In the midst of the pleasantries, Mayor Pei appeared to be both excited and nervous. He led Judge Dee into a spacious room, which looked like a comfortable combination of a library and a home office.

Apparently, Mayor Pei had also made it something of a cozy retreat for himself. Its mahogany-framed lattice windows showed elegant designs against the white walls, which were lined with well-stocked dark wood bookshelves, decorated here and there with choice antique bowls and vases. The long ebony desk was topped with black-streaked white marble, on which stood a large porcelain vase sporting a bouquet of yellow chrysanthemums, two or three days old, thinner, but still attractive.

The two of them seated themselves in the red damask-cushioned chairs with a tall tea stand between them.

'In accordance with our yellow lunar calendar, Your Honor, today is a day marked as an auspicious one. For me, a lot of things have been going badly of late. I hope your visit may miraculously turn the luck for me.'

Mayor Pei was a sharp one in spite of his bookish appearance, who immediately came to the realization that Judge Dee would not have come all the way over for a long-time-no-see chit-chat early in the morning.

'In this red-dust world of ours, eight or nine times out of ten, things do not go the way we expect,' Judge Dee said, quoting an ancient saying in the Han dynasty. 'There is no smooth sailing all the time.'

'So please tell me, Your Honor, what favorable wind has brought you over to my place today?'

'To open the door to the mountains, Your Excellency, I have to admit that it is the wind of the Xuanji case. It has become such a sensational one.'

'Yes, an extremely sensational case indeed.'

'I was about to leave the capital for another post, as you may have learned, when Internal Minister Wu asked me to take a look into the murder case before setting out for the trip. So I'm just taking a quick look for him. It's not in any official capacity, needless to say.'

'Internal Minister Wu! But that's little wonder. He admires your talent so much as the most capable judge of the Great Tang Empire. For the murder investigation, your help will be like the long-expected rain during a summer drought. Not just for the minister, but for me, too. It may truly turn the luck for me. So please go ahead with any questions you have about the murder case. And any suggestions and directions from you will be very much appreciated.'

'To begin with, the murder case has not yet been concluded in spite of Xuanji's confession, Mayor Pei?'

'No, not yet. Under normal circumstances, after a murder suspect such as Xuanji pleads guilty, it's just a matter of time for the approval of execution to come from the higher authorities. But you may have heard of the way she pleaded guilty, and then of the outcries about it from a group of men of letters – some of them quite well known and influential – declaring that she was tortured into the confession. So it's understandable for Minister Wu to seek your help. After all, the case should not drag on like this for such a long time.'

'That's true.' Judge Dee took a sip of the tea, waiting for Pei to go on.

Without beating around the bush, Pei began by defending the way he had conducted the recent trial.

'Let me say something first, Your Honor. When Xuanji was initially brought into the courtroom, she was so defiant, so uncooperative. She kept declaring she did not know anything about the death of her maidservant Ning. There was no accepting her statement just like that, as you understand. You have done quite a number of trials yourself. In the courtroom, I had to subject her to a beating, as is conventional. Obviously, most of the Tang officials are not that qualified as judges, not as experienced, resourceful as you. But that's as much as I could possibly do to fulfill my judicial responsibility. People may have all sorts of speculations about the trial, but they're not true.'

'No, I'm not that experienced or resourceful as a judge. The civil service examination requires nothing but our studies of the Confucian classics. There's not a single book about the judicial system requested in school. I have been trying to maneuver the best I could in the gray area all these years.'

'You are just so extraordinary. No one will argue about it, Judge Dee. But back to people's speculations about the case – there's something I have to say. Months before the murder case, I had tried to invite Xuanji to one of my parties. It's because Zi'an's wife is a distant cousin of mine, and I had heard about her harshness toward Xuanji. So I merely wanted to do something for her – by way of compensation. For a courtesan like Xuanji, the larger her network, the better. She might have met some interesting, influential people at the party at my place. But she responded with a flat no, which I could understand. She is a proud woman in her way, and I bore her no grudge. Period.

'But because of it, others may have seen me as a man going after her, and even as one rejected by her in the light of her refusal of my party invitation. That led to the false assumption that the trial was done in an unfair way, even a matter of retaliation by torturing her into confession in prison.'

'I understand, Mayor Pei. With a suspect refusing to own up, I would have done the same thing in the courtroom. Indeed, how could she have claimed that she savagely beat the maidservant to death and buried her in the backyard in a drunken stupor without knowing anything about it?'

'Exactly. It did not make any sense, did it?'

'No, it did not. But she then made a modified statement in prison, didn't she?'

'But what do you think of the second statement, Your Honor?'

'There're quite a number of holes in her second statement, too. To begin with, it's possible for her to get blind drunk, but to kill someone without a conscious motive or reason is simply too incredible.'

'You can say that again,' Mayor Pei said, nodding vigorously. 'With the far-from-admissible "confession" made by her in prison, with the men of letters clamoring that she simply gave in to the horrible torture in the prison cell, and at the same time, with people high above pressing for a speedy yet acceptable conclusion, I'm really at my wits' end.'

'What is an acceptable conclusion? Indeed, it's such a tough case for you. As it seems to me, Mayor Pei, the crux of the matter for you is how to get a truthful, convincing confession from her. In that event, those men of letters would clamor no more, and the people above, whoever they might be, would no longer have the pretext to push. Things would then become acceptable to the people concerned.'

'But how, my celebrated Judge Dee? She will not say anything more, and I cannot give her another beating in the courtroom, nor in the prison cell. Already so many protests and complaints have popped up like crazy cicadas screeching non-stop in the summer.' Pei added after a short pause, 'Has Minister Wu discussed the case with you?'

'He sent me a brief case report, but it sheds little light on the complexities of the case. There're a lot of unanswered questions in it.'

'Last night, I restudied her second statement. It's practically as unconvincing as the first one. Furthermore, whatever changes were made in that statement, it makes no difference for the conclusion of the case. It still spells the death sentence for her.'

'Perhaps she cannot bear it in the prison cell any longer. She, too, wants a quick conclusion – death sentence or not. She came up with what she considered a more convincing confession, so you would have the case closed.'

'That may be true.'

'Alternatively, she could have tried to cover up something or somebody with such a conclusion of the murder case.'

'Have something or somebody covered up?' Mayor Pei repeated the question. 'Now you mention it, some people above did talk to me about the urgency of getting to the very bottom of it, and bringing the people involved to justice, whatever their position or status. That's what was said to me, I remember – something to that effect, at least.'

It was the third time that Pei mentioned 'some people above,' who must have an undisclosed reason to bring pressure to bear upon the mayor like that.

A shudder ran down through Judge Dee's spine. It confirmed the scenario he had contemplated the previous night, the more so in the light of the peony poem written by Xuanji. And it was the very poem delivered by the flower girl the night before.

'What specifically do you mean by "some people above," Your Excellency?'

'Well, I'm just a low-level mayor on the outskirts of the capital,' Mayor Pei said, abruptly sounding evasive again. 'There're so many people high above in the great capital, demanding this and that, as you may well imagine.'

'Just as the old saying goes, "It's so difficult to serve as an official in the capital." There're so many people high above you here. That's why I have no choice but to leave.'

'Come on, Your Honor. You're one of those most trusted by Her Majesty. You don't have to say that to me. But it's true:

it's far more difficult to serve as an official on the outskirts of the great capital, with far more people high above.'

'And with the case dragging on, bringing about more and more collateral damage—'

'What do you mean by "more collateral damage," Your Honor?'

'Have you heard of the death of Wei, Mayor Pei?'

'Wei, the good-for-nothing man connected to Xuanji?'

'Yes, he was killed yesterday afternoon on the road in front of the nunnery. According to some villagers there, Wei's the man kept by her in a hut she purchased for him.'

'Oh, I did not know anything because I did not go to the office yesterday. Is there anything – any details – you happen to know about the killing of Wei near the nunnery?'

'Possibly a chance mugging that went wrong. But I doubt it. Wei did not make a likely target. And it happened in broad daylight, too. According to a villager who hurried out to the crime scene a little later, catching only a glance of the back of a black-attired rider galloping out of sight, Wei was killed with something like a saber. The attacker delivered two or three vicious swipes from the black horse.'

'A black-attired rider on a black horse! I'll be damned, Your Honor. It's getting more and more weird and complicated. I'll check into it this morning. So you think Wei's death is related to Xuanji's case?'

'Wei's closely related to Xuanji, no question about it. And there's another death possibly related to the murder case, I'm afraid.'

'Another death related to the Xuanji case – when did it happen?'

'Last night. The young flower girl surnamed Zhang, who had a flower garden at the southern end of the village, was killed on the mountain trail not far from the village.'

'But how was she connected to Xuanji?'

'Xuanji frequented her flower garden for bouquets at her poetry parties in the nunnery. In fact, Xuanji took her under her wing as something like a protégée and confidante.'

'How was the flower girl killed?'

'She was attacked on the trail. According to some villagers

who discovered her body afterward, it was possibly a sex crime that went wrong with scratches and bruises on her body, and with her clothes badly torn.'

'A sex crime at night in the village neighborhood?'

'It's unbelievable, isn't it?' Judge Dee paused theatrically before he went on. 'And there's something more unbelievable. Among Xuanji's best-known poems, one is titled, "To a Girl in the Neighborhood."'

'Yes, I think I've heard of it.'

'That very poem is about the flower girl in question. So in the course of a single day, with two people connected to Xuanji killed, you cannot help feeling alarmed. What about others connected to her, too?'

'That's more than alarming, Your Honor. The list of the people Xuanji's associated with could be quite long. So the collateral damage—'

'The list of collateral damage could also turn out to be quite long. And the pressure for a quick breakthrough and conclusion is mounting in the meantime. In the event of more victims and no breakthrough in sight, I don't know what may happen.'

The mayor stood up in spite of himself. A spell of silence ensued in the room.

'As you have mentioned, the crux of the matter is a speedy conclusion with an acceptable confession on the part of Xuanji, which is something beyond me. I've tried my best, but without any success,' Mayor Pei finally resumed. 'Since you're here today, why don't you try to talk to her? She must have heard such a lot about you, our celebrated Judge Dee, and you, of all people, may succeed in making her spill out the truth.'

Mayor Pei might not have been too pleased with Judge Dee's involvement in the investigation, but the mayor had no choice, as he knew only too well.

'No, it's your case, Mayor Pei. I don't think Her Majesty would be too pleased with my cooking in other people's kitchen.'

'But it would be a different story with others failing to produce anything satisfactory in that kitchen. Not to mention the fact that it's a request from Minister Wu.'

That was probably a well-calculated probe from Mayor Pei, but it was also an opportunity Judge Dee thought he had to seize.

'If you really insist, I would not mind giving it a try, but I cannot guarantee anything, Mayor Pei.' He then added, as if as an afterthought, 'I've read quite a lot of her poems, so I think she may at least tell me something about her work, and possibly about her life behind it – if nothing else – from a one-to-one talk in person.'

'Yes, you have written a number of poems yourself. That will most likely make her willing to talk to you. Not just as Judge Dee, but as Poet Dee, too.'

'I'm not a poet beside her. But just between you and me, I have been toying with the idea of compiling a collection of her poetry.'

'A poetry collection – what a novel idea! And a practical one as well. With an in-depth discussion with her about her works, yours could soon prove to be the one and only authorized edition,' Mayor Pei said with a broad grin. 'A visit to her prison cell could be arranged for you right at this very moment.'

Judge Dee had visited prisons before on a variety of occasions. This would probably turn out to be one of the most depressing visits. He found himself immersed in dismal anticipation, what with Xuanji's tragic life story, and with the inevitable doom looming against her in the background.

Yang followed his master, looking around on high alert and grasping the hilt of the saber fastened by his side.

The prison guard was a tall, gaunt man surnamed Huang, who looked to be in his mid-fifties. The moment Judge Dee handed him the handwritten note from Mayor Pei as well as the authorization letter from Internal Minister Wu, Huang knelt down on the dirty ground in haste and kowtowed non-stop like a prisoner there.

'Your visit today is bringing the greatest honor to the sordid prison, Your Excellency.'

'I'm here because of a possible poetry collection for Xuanji. So I'll be talking to her alone. You don't have to say anything about it to other people, of course.'

'Absolute privacy, I understand, Your Excellency. You may talk to her as long as you like. In fact, you are the only one Mayor Pei has granted permission to go in and visit her here. As people are all saying, she's the black fox spirit incarnate, capable of causing horrible harm to those who come close to her. We cannot be too careful.'

'You don't have to worry about that for my master,' Yang cut in with undisguised scorn in his voice. 'He's a man of such noble integrity that evil spirits could do him no harm.'

'Oh, you may run an errand for me, Yang,' Judge Dee said to his loyal assistant. 'Go and buy a decent basket of lunch for Xuanji and me. And a kettle of mellow yellow rice wine, too. It may be a long talk, and it will soon be lunchtime.'

'Yes, it will be lunchtime soon. You need to take care of yourself, too, Master.'

As Yang was about to leave, Judge Dee turned abruptly to stop him. 'Also, go to Mayor Pei's residence first for a search warrant for both the hut and the nunnery. Bring in whatever strikes you as suspicious or unusual.'

'I'll do a thorough search both in the hut and the nunnery, Master.'

'And one more thing, bring over the yellow silk underrobe to me as well upon your return. I have left it in a mahogany box in the carriage outside. And a bouquet of peonies.'

'Yes, the yellow silk underrobe embroidered with golden dragons. As for the peonies, what color?'

'It does not matter. You pick whatever color is available. And don't worry about the expense.'

With Yang withdrawing out of sight, Judge Dee turned to Huang,

'People cannot be too careful; I couldn't agree with you more. Now, a couple of questions for you first, Huang.'

'Yes, anything you want to know, Your Excellency.'

'Has anyone else come to visit her in the prison cell here?'

'Nobody except the mayor himself, and he was here just one time, but he did not stay long. Nor did he step inside her cell. I had to drag her out to the prison office for the meeting.'

'Has anyone else tried to contact her or send her things or messages?'

'Not that I know of, Your Excellency. Certainly, nothing like a basket of lunch or a bouquet of peonies.'

'Has she said anything to you about the case?'

'She's broken, literally broken, washing her face with tears all day long. And she has hardly spoken a complete sentence to me.'

While talking, Judge Dee followed Huang through the narrow corridor with darksome, squalid cells lined along both sides – some occupied with prisoners, some vacant – toward the end of the corridor which presented a more somber cell like a deserted enclave on the right. That was a single cell for Xuanji.

It might be just as well. At least he did not have to worry about being observed or overheard in his meeting, discussing the case with her.

Still several steps away from the cell door, he was greeted with an unpleasant stench issuing from the cell.

Looking through the enveloping dimness, he managed to make out a slender figure lying on something like a heap of straw and rags, which apparently served as a bed for her. The musty-smelling, oppressive-looking cell was littered with nondescript rubbish under the crumbling walls. Except for a small bamboo stool and a black wooden chamber pot, there was no other furniture in the cell.

Huang hurried ahead of Judge Dee and unlocked the brass padlock with a clang.

Stepping into the cell, Judge Dee was shocked at the sight of Xuanji lying with her face turned to the wall, and with her back bare – practically all the way down to her bare feet.

It was obvious that she had not washed for days. A repulsive odor came from her sullied body, possibly from the rotten straw, too. His glance moved down and noted her dirty, almost black, soles; she must have been moving barefoot all the time since she had been in prison.

She seemed to have difficulty turning slowly over to him, with her hands and feet still in black iron chains. He found himself staring at a young woman who had a haggard yet still attractive face, even with smudges and bruises. She appeared so fragile, vulnerable in something like a sleeveless wrap of rough material, suggestive of a piece of cloth tossed over the front of her naked body at random, secured by only a straw belt along the waist, leaving her back entirely uncovered.

At a candlelight masquerade party in the nunnery, such exotic attire – if 'attire' was the word for it – could have been seen as surrealistically sexy, but in the squalid cell, it merely added to the sordidness of the scene.

And to his horror, the wrap appeared badly torn around her left shoulder, revealing some crisscrossing welt-like streaks, as if painted in scarlet, which must have been inflicted after she was thrown in prison.

What she would have really looked like as a celebrated poetess at those glamorous poetry parties in the nunnery, Judge Dee failed to imagine.

'You don't have any prison clothes for her?' Judge Dee said to Huang, knitting his brow over the scene. 'After all, she is such a renowned poetess.'

'No, we had no choice, Your Excellency,' Huang said in a hesitant whisper. 'She was carried into the cell unconscious, with her thighs and buttocks still badly bleeding after the brutal bludgeoning at the courtroom. Had we put any clothing on her, it could have hurt more terribly with her skin stuck to fabric with dried blood. So we improvised like that. We managed to have her lying on her stomach, and her back uncovered, so the wounds could heal a little quicker. Fortunately, the weather has been relatively warm for the last few days.'

'Bring a doctor to the prison immediately – wait, no, immediately after I leave. She should have her wounds treated as soon as possible, and as properly as possible, and then have some proper clothing made for her here.'

'But somebody from above gave the order that she should be treated just like other prisoners – no special treatment whatsoever. You may guess what an order like this could mean, Your Excellency.'

'Well, tell "somebody from above" that I have ordered you to do so. If anything happens because of it, I will be held responsible.'

The talk with the prison guard must have given the judge

away, making it impossible for Judge Dee to present himself to her merely as a scholar interested in the compilation of a poetry collection, but he did not think he could make much use of such a cover in her presence.

Recognizing his authoritative air, she sat up, trying to pull down the wrap to cover her soiled legs and feet, but it was an unsuccessful attempt.

'Stay outside, Huang. I will call you if I need you.' He then added, 'Oh, go and bring in a basin of hot water and clean towels.'

The moment Huang withdrew from the cell, Xuanji said in a feeble voice, 'Forgive me for presenting my pathetic self to you at such a place, Your Excellency.'

'You don't have to say that, Xuanji. Let me introduce myself. I'm Dee Renjie. People sometimes call me Judge Dee, but I also write poems. As a fan of your poems, I would like to compile a special collection of the poems composed by you, Wen, and possibly Zi'an too – that is, if I can get hold of enough of his works. I've talked to Mayor Pei, a former colleague of mine, about such a possibility, and he suggested that I have a talk with you here to double-check the circumstances in which some of the poems were composed.'

'Thank you so much for your interest in my poetry, Your Honor. And you're the first visitor to step into the squalid prison cell, which I appreciate from the bottom of my heart. For poetry or not, Mayor Pei would never have set foot inside the prison cell.'

'But I would like to say one good word for Mayor Pei, Xuanji. I have just had a talk with him. According to him, he once tried to invite you to his party because Zi'an's wife, a distant cousin of his, had behaved in such an unfair way to you. He simply wanted to offer a sort of compensation—'

'What's the point of saying all that to me at present, Your Honor?'

'Mayor Pei feels so sorry about what happened to you in the courtroom, but he had no choice because of your unacceptable statement about the murder case. Not just with the first statement, but with the second one made in the prison as well. As a mayor, he's supposed to go on with the interrogation, giving you another beating, and then still another, until you finally come to tell the truth – an admissible, convincing confession about the murder, an acceptable statement in which people will no longer be able to find so many holes.'

'What can I do if others choose not to believe me? You are the celebrated Judge Dee, you tell me what—'

It was then that the cell door was elbowed open again.

Huang returned, holding a large wooden basin of warm water in both hands along with three or four clean towels draped on his right arm.

'That's a good job, Huang. Remove the chains from her wrists and ankles. You don't have to worry about anything. She can hardly walk right now.'

'Whatever you wish, Your Excellency.'

Huang did what he was told before he stood up obsequiously in expectation.

'You may leave now, Huang. I, too, want to step out with you for a breath of fresh air. It's a bit too stuffy in here for an old man like me. Take your time, Xuanji. I'll be back in a while.'

It was after quite some time that Judge Dee returned to the foul-smelling cell.

But Xuanji looked like a different woman, her hair tied with a scrap of rag, her face still so pale, wan, but with the smudges wiped away. She was not without a suggestion of her once vivacious beauty.

The water in the wooden basin at her feet also appeared different – of a sordid black color – like a footnote to the metamorphosis in the prison cell.

She blushed, struggled up with difficulty, knelt down on the dirty, damp floor, and kowtowed to Judge Dee.

He hastened to help her back to the heap of straw. From the opening of her wrap, he caught a glimpse of a rivulet of sweat leaving a light black streak in the hollow of her bosom again, as he perched himself on the squeaky bamboo stool opposite in the suffocating cell.

'I'm sorry about what has happened to you, Xuanji. I've read so many of your poems with admiration. How I wish I could write like you! Your poem "To Zi'an, Looking out across Han River in Sorrow" is such a masterpiece indeed:

'Myriads of maple leaves
upon myriads of maple leaves
silhouetted against the bridge,
a few white sails return late in the dusk.

How do I miss you?

My thoughts of you run
like the water in the West River,
flowing eastward, never-ending,
day and night.'

'You don't have to say that to me, Your Honor. Poetry can make nothing happen in this world of red dust. You've just read that piece written to Zi'an, but he has not even sent a short message to me in the prison here.'

'What a shame!'

'Like others, I've heard so much about your brilliant work as a capable and honest official, Your Honor. My days are numbered; I know that only too well. There's no point beating about the bush. Apart from all the empty talk about poetry, what else can people really do with an ill-starred woman like me?'

Apparently, Xuanji was too intelligent to believe that he came to the prison for the sake of poetry.

'Yours appears to be a very complicated case, but let me first make one thing clear. I'm here not in any official position to investigate your case. Having said that, I admit that I'm not that unfamiliar with it. It's because quite a number of people have talked to me about it.'

'I'm not surprised, Your Honor.'

'I like your poems, that's true, but there are far more things than poetry can possibly tell in this world. So regarding my questions about your poems – and about the case, too – let me start at the very beginning.'

It was going to be a shot in the dark, but Judge Dee did not think he would have the time for one of those usual approaches he had taken before.

'Just three days ago, I was leaving the capital of Chang'an for a new post in another province when Internal Minister Wu sent a messenger to me in a hostel at night, asking me to take a look into your case.'

'Internal Minister Wu?'

'Yes. I, too, was more than confounded. As an old-fashioned man, I recently submitted a memorial to the empress about keeping the crown prince of the Li family in line for succession, for which Minister Wu could not but see me as an obstacle to his own ambition for the throne. So why would he have requested my help for your murder case?'

'That also puzzles me. Minister Wu wants to succeed the empress – that's no secret under the sun of the Tang Empire. Then, why should he have been so anxious for your help in an ordinary murder case like mine?'

Xuanji seemed to be well informed about the power struggle at the court, though it was perhaps not too much of a surprise for someone with her wide connections.

'According to Minister Wu, your case has stirred up a lot of controversies in the empire, so much so that it might come to affect its political stability. As a result, I had to agree to take a look into it. To my consternation, Minister Wu was not pushing me alone. Mayor Pei, too, has told me that he's under a lot of pressure from above to investigate further.'

'Really!'

'Yes. "Get to the very bottom of it, and bring everybody involved to justice, whatever his position or status." Those are the exact words said to Mayor Pei from somebody high above. So, you see, Internal Minister Wu must have suspected that somebody else is involved in the case.'

'Somebody else?'

'I'm afraid so. There are all sorts of questions about how you could have pulled it off by yourself. Not just the murder, but the burial of the body, too. And it's a legitimate question: How could a young, delicate woman like you have done that job single-handedly? With questions like that remaining unanswered, Mayor Pei and the people above him will have no choice but to go all the way, by hook or by crook, to get what they want from you. It's just a matter of time before some clues come to the surface—'

'But I was so drunk, Your Honor. I did not remember anything about what happened in the nunnery that night. Whatever I may choose to say now, people will still have their doubts about it.'

'Let me put it this way, Xuanji. As something of a judge, I, too, have questions about the case, though I have not yet discussed them with others – neither with Mayor Pei nor with Internal Minister Wu.'

'What are your questions?'

'Well, let's establish a clear timeline first, and we can talk about things in the proper order. Ning's body was discovered on the third day of the month, and earlier that day you had a lunch party with several guests. However, Ning was killed the day before, the second day of the month, when you entertained a very special guest in the evening, about which you did not say anything to Mayor Pei.'

'What are you saying?' she said, her face instantly bleached of color. 'I had no party or a guest on the evening of the second day of the month. I was drunk, as I've told you.'

'That's why we have to begin from the very beginning, Xuanji. On the morning of the second day, you went out shopping, purchasing a lot of fancy and expensive stuff. And a large bouquet of peonies from the flower girl Zhang in the village as well. According to her, you picked up flowers only when you had a special guest or party. So that really shed light on your unusual purchases that day.'

'That morning, Ning told me that she had to go back home for a day or two, so I did the shopping by myself for the party scheduled for the next day. How could that have anything to do with the murder case, Your Honor?'

'For one thing, your shopping list included swallow saliva nest and shark fin, but in very small quantities – enough only for one person. The store owner said you bargained with him, saying you had just one guest that evening.'

'I cannot remember what I said exactly to the store owner,

but I might have made up something like that, so he would not insist on selling the whole box to me. Both the swallow saliva nest and the shark fin are ridiculously expensive, you know.'

'And there were also live fish and shrimp – in very small quantities, too – in your shopping basket. Usually, people make a point of preparing and cooking them live. So how could you have purchased them for the party the next day – with the fish and shrimp long dead?'

'I did not buy all of them for the party the next day. Some I just wanted to treat myself to in the evening. Ning was a capable servant, but not a gourmet chef.'

'But in your statement, shortly after you got back from the shopping trip, you started drinking by yourself instead of preparing the live fish and shrimp. That did not add up, Xuanji.'

She failed to produce a response, murmuring an indistinct word or two and shaking her head in confusion.

'As a judge, I cannot help coming up with different scenarios, which may or may not necessarily prove to be one hundred percent true. Quite likely, they're nothing but fantasies conjured up, I have to admit, in the feeble brain of an old man during sleepless nights. No offense, Xuanji – that's just in the line of my work,' Judge Dee said, stretching his legs, feeling increasingly uncomfortable sitting in the same position on the bamboo stool. 'Now, instead of going into the questions one by one, I think I'll start by presenting a couple of scenarios to you.'

'You have more than one scenario?'

'For the first one, let's suppose Ning not only stayed in the nunnery when you came back from shopping, but she also said or did something outrageous to you. Totally intolerable. Flying into an uncontrollable rage, you started kicking and whipping at her with all your strength, not stopping until she sank to the floor. She died there and then, and it's too late for you to do anything about it. It's possible you were not really aware, as you've said, of what you were doing at the time, as you were overwhelmed by a blinding fury. In another case I dealt with several years ago, I encountered something like that—'

'I don't know what you are talking about, Your Honor.'

'In this scenario, the sequence might be complicated. But

let's suppose that somebody arrived at the nunnery before Ning left for home. Who could have made such an unannounced visit? Wei? He's a regular visitor, also an impossible womanizer, and Ning was a coquettish young girl. So what could the two have done there while you were away shopping?

'Upon your return, you found Ning still there, half-clad, disheveled – busy erasing suspicious traces in the bedroom. It took no brains to know what had just happened between Wei and Ning. You were precipitated into a fit of murderous fury, and I don't think I need to go into details here about what then took place there. Later, Wei came back over to the nunnery. And he helped you bury Ning's body in the night. The shocking discovery of the body the next day, however, had you thrown into prison. With the murder investigation dragging on, Wei became more and more worried about the possibility of your giving him up as the accomplice that night. That accounted for his sudden flight yesterday.'

'What do you mean by "his sudden flight yesterday," Your Honor?'

'I've not finished yet, Xuanji. Such a scenario may account for several aspects of the case, and it sheds light on the circumstances of the flight as well as the subsequent death – the second death—'

'The second death . . .'

'Yes, the death of Wei!'

'What! Wei died?'

'He died yesterday.'

She looked up sharply. A faint spot of color seemed to be returning to her cheeks, though her face was otherwise still mask-like and betraying no emotion.

'Forsooth, I'm cursed beyond redemption!'

'What do you mean, Xuanji?'

'I'm really cursed with the black fox spirit, as the villagers have declared, so those people close to me also suffer the worst luck imaginable.'

'No, I don't believe so. Confucius says, "A gentleman does not talk about spirits and ghosts." Whatever interpretation, however, it's hard not to associate the two deaths, each of them connected to you in one way or another.'

'I did not know anything about Wei's death, Your Honor, not until you mentioned it just now.'

'That I believe. You were here. In fact, Mayor Pei has not yet heard anything about it, either. My assistant did a hurried search at the crime scene, so I can tell you some details about it. According to an eyewitness there, shortly after noon-time, Wei broke into the nunnery, packed up valuables into a gray cloth bundle, and sneaked out. Carrying the large bundle on his back, he was fleeing down to the road that stretches out in front of the nunnery, when out of the blue a horseman rushed over, caught up with him from behind, and struck out with a saber. Wei was killed with two mighty slashes at the head and shoulder, and a vicious thrust in the groin. The large bundle on his back was gone when his body was discovered by the roadside.

'But why should Wei have tried to flee like that? That's a question we have to answer. So far, Wei has not been seen even as a suspect. Mayor Pei has not so much as sent for him as a witness. While your being locked up here did not help him financially, it could be much worse in the event of his moving somewhere else. At least the hut here was rent-free for him. Besides, who would have ambushed a penniless, harmless man like Wei?'

She opened her mouth, but said nothing.

'To be frank, anything would have been possible for a man like Wei, Xuanji. But from another perspective, the dead take secrets into the grave, just like the old saying.'

In spite of herself, she started fidgeting on the heap of straw. An eerie noise became audible, like a rat's feet scurrying over the cell floor scattered with stray straw. He wondered whether she got the hint in his last sentence.

'Could that have been a mugging gone wrong?' she said weakly. 'Perhaps it was because of the cloth bundle he carried on his back.'

'No, I'm not inclined toward the theory of a screwed-up mugging. A bundle-carrying man was a common sight along the road. Who could tell what was inside the bundle? Besides, it's not a likely location for a mugging, particularly not during the day, nor with Wei as a likely target. The killer must have been waiting there to ambush him.'

'It's possible,' she finally said.

It was the first time she agreed with anything Judge Dee had said.

'And there's something so inexplicable about the way Wei was attacked.'

'What's so inexplicable, Your Honor?'

'The two hits at the head and shoulder must have finished him instantly. Then why inflict the stab to the groin? The killer had to dismount for him to do so. Not unless it was done for a specific message, the way I read it, about his having touched an untouchable woman . . .'

Their talk was once again interrupted, this time by Yang who was moving across the corridor in strides toward the prison cell, carrying a vermillion-painted bamboo lunch box in one hand and a fairly large bag in another.

Judge Dee stood up shakily, his feet and legs numbed from sitting too long on the small bamboo stool, unable to stretch out in the cramped cell space.

Pushing open the unlocked cell door with his elbow, Yang put down the bag and the two-tiered bamboo box on the ground. The box contained four or five dainty dishes, and a kettle of amber-colored sticky rice wine. Squatting, he tried to find a piece of board on which to place the cups and dishes, yet without success. He ended up turning over the box lid, which served as a tiny tabletop between Judge Dee and Xuanji.

'Thanks, Yang. You have done a good job. Now you may leave. And I, too, have to stand up and stretch my legs a little,' Judge Dee said, rising to see Yang off in a ceremonious way, but making half a step out of the prison cell.

Yang looked around, turned, and started whispering excitedly into his master's ears.

'Got you,' Judge Dee said simply after he listened through the briefing from his assistant, his one foot still remaining in the prison cell.

Turning back into the cell, Judge Dee poured out a cup of the slightly sweet sticky rice wine for Xuanji.

'I did not know things could be so horrible in the prison. So at least we should have a decent meal, if nothing else. It's about all my assistant Yang could have done at such short notice. Sorry, nothing fancy like shark fin—'

'You really don't have to say that, Your Honor.'

So saying, she crawled over to the lunch basket and snatched up a chunk of wood-smoked Sichuan duck with her swollen fingers. She looked nothing like a graceful poetess in those elegant images of her poetry.

'The finger-crunching torture in prison, as you probably know,' she said with a sarcastic smile when she saw Judge Dee staring at her hands. 'Anyway, I can hardly hold chopsticks nowadays.'

It was little wonder, Judge Dee contemplated in the surrounding gloom, aware of all the cruel tortures she had endured here.

She was licking a finger that was without its fingernail – possibly pulled away by force. Those rumors about the torture in prison were not unfounded. He could not help wondering whether the cruel torture had also been ordered by somebody 'high above' Mayor Pei.

All the pressure had been given, presumably, for a conclusion in the interests of those people around the throne, and, at the same time, acceptable to the public who did not know anything about the politics behind the scene.

'What were you saying, Your Honor?' she said after having devoured more than half of the dainty dishes placed on the bamboo basket lid.

Perhaps she was now ready to say something. Not because of the lunch, Judge Dee observed, sipping at his cup. The sticky rice wine went smoothly down his throat.

'I was talking about a couple of possible scenarios. The first one, with Wei as the accomplice that night, answers some of the questions, but it also leaves quite a number of them unanswered, and gives rise to others as well. For starters, Wei had not even been summoned by Mayor Pei, so why should he have tried to flee all of a sudden, with nothing but a bundle on his back? Here, he had a hut under his name, not to mention those connections of yours, and some of them may help him out because of you. More importantly, nobody else knew that Wei was the accomplice in the murder case, so who would have gone so far as to kill him?'

'But how could I know all that, Your Honor?'

'And to make a hypothesis for the sake of making a hypothesis, Wei was attacked because his tryst with Ning became known to one of her other lovers. But that does not sound plausible. No, not at all.'

'You are the celebrated judge, not me.' She then added reflectively, 'He was a womanizer – you're absolutely right about it. As far as I know, he slept with other married women in town. One of the cuckolded husbands could have got wind of it and killed him in revenge.'

It was strange the way she was speaking, as if more than willing to offer a scenario echoing Judge Dee's, more or less in that direction.

'With questions like those unanswered, I began working on the second scenario. It may appear to be even more strange than the first one, Xuanji – pretty much guesswork based on a variety of pieces seemingly irrelevant to the whole puzzle. But it's a scenario that accounts not only for Wei's flight but also for the attempt at his life.

'And it accounts for the ultimate mystery behind this bizarre case, too.'

'Is that so, Your Honor?'

Standing up from the stool, he bent over, opened the bag on the ground, and pulled out a head-to-foot costume with a dramatic wave of his hand like a magician at a market fair – a black fox costume, made of some hairy, fluffy material and with a long trembling tail.

'What the devil is that ghastly stuff you are showing me, Your Honor?'

'The very black fox spirit that scared the shit out of the villagers. My assistant Yang has just found it in Wei's hut with the search warrant from Mayor Pei. Not exactly what I anticipated, but nonetheless a random harvest. It helps to shed some light on the existence of the black fox spirit in the neighborhood of the nunnery – particularly on its mysteriously intensified movement of late.'

'It's nothing but a stupid supernatural tale among those ignorant village folk,' she said, her fingers clutching the black fox costume spasmodically in spite of herself. 'An absurd superstitious belief. What on the earth does the black fox costume have to do with that second scenario of yours?'

'As an investigator, I have no choice but to check and double-check all the aspects possibly related to the case. According to several village folk, you're simply bewitched out of your mind by the black fox spirit, and that's why you killed the maid in a fit of madness. Period. They're also emphatic that the nunnery was haunted by the black fox spirit, particularly for the last couple of months. A number of villagers testified to me and my assistant that they saw with their own eyes the fox spirit skulking around, though you seemed not to have been bothered by the apparition at all.'

'What are you driving at, Your Honor? How could I have been so superstitious as to be bothered by the stupid speculation among the village folk?'

'Had it been just one or two villagers peddling such wild stories, I would not have given any credit to it. But there were quite a few villagers, and some of them swore that they actually saw the black fox spirit more than one time. I had to take it seriously.

'Wei's nocturnal movements in the vicinity of the nunnery could have led to the neighborhood people imagining things, finger-pointing, gossiping, and speculating. It was understandable that he felt bugged, so the black fox costume could have been designed for a specific purpose: to make the black fox spirit even more realistically menacing so as to scare the village folk away. Consequently, they would not be able to witness his visits to you in the nunnery.

'But then a question follows, Xuanji. Wei had been seeing you for quite a long time, so why had he not tried to do anything about it until just about a month and a half ago? Besides, his wearing the black fox costume for his visits at night could also have escalated the spreading of the black fox stories, and that could have been something unpleasant to you.'

'I've had no idea at all about the existence of the black fox costume, Your Honor, let alone its specific purpose. I'm totally befuddled. You were talking about the death of Wei. Then why, all of a sudden, the abrupt shift to the black fox costume or the black fox spirit?'

'Because it has everything to do with the death of Wei,

Xuanji. Paradoxically, the second scenario, which involves the black fox spirit in such a superstitious way, has evolved out of the first scenario.

'As I've mentioned earlier, on the second day of the month, you made elaborate, extravagant preparations for dinner in expectation of a mysterious guest in the evening. Such expensive delicacies as swallow saliva nest and shark fin were not purchased for a low-class man like Wei, I am guessing, but for a man of really high social status.'

'Almost all the visitors to me at the nunnery are of higher social status than Wei. That does not really mean anything, Your Honor.'

'But much, much higher social status, I have to say, than all of the visitors you have received there. Guess how the flower girl Zhang described the mysterious man you were seeing for the last couple of months? She said you compared him to "a divine dragon soaring in the cloud, with its head visible, but not with its tail." It's something you have never said about any man before, so she remembered.'

'Zhang is a young, naïve girl who has a knack for exaggeration. The chit-chat between the two of us should not have been taken too seriously.'

'Alas, Zhang was silenced.'

'What do you mean, Your Honor?'

'She, too, was killed yesterday – in the evening. Mayor Pei and I have just had a discussion about it. To say the least, we could not rule out the possibility of her death being related to your case. First Wei and then the flower girl Zhang. Killed in the same day.'

'Oh, it's such a shock, and very sad, but I was just one of her customers at the flower garden.'

'Definitely more than "just one" of her customers; you know that, Xuanji – the way you talked to her about the special guest you were seeing. Not to mention the poem you wrote for her – "To a Girl in the Neighborhood." Again, according to the flower girl, it's rather unusual that she had been barred from entering the nunnery for the last couple of months. Why all the secrecy all of a sudden for a close confidante like her? Supposing the special guest is a married man – but what's the problem with that? Most of the visitors to the nunnery are married. It's no big deal, and I agreed with the flower girl on that.'

'One more piece of collateral damage. I was truly born under an ill star—'

Her sentence was cut short with the eerie sound of something black jumping, bumping against the rusted window railing of the cell, as if in support of the superstitious belief of the black fox spirit. They turned toward the window in haste, but they failed to see anything there.

Could that be another ominous sign?

'Oh, it's nothing,' Judge Dee said in relief. 'You were talking about the curse of the black fox spirit. No, you had just denied its existence. And I agree with you that it's nothing but superstitious belief among the village folk. On the other hand, it's really because of the complexities of the case that the black fox spirit came into the picture. I've discussed some of these complexities with Mayor Pei, but not all of them.'

'You are scaring me, Your Honor!'

'No, I'm not. But I'm very much worried that with the case dragging on like this, more collateral damage will come. Wei might not have been innocent, but the young flower girl was different, and I feel so sorry about her. Had she not come to deliver the poem to me in the temple, she might not have been ambushed on the mountain path. It would probably just have been a matter of time before the killer silenced her one way or another, though.

'So the list of collateral damage could prove to be long. After Wei and the flower girl, other people connected to you – even though not that closely – would be removed as well. Those "high above" are just like Cao Cao, the mighty prime minister of the Han dynasty, who declared that he would rather wrong all the people in the world than let himself be wronged by others.'

A ghastly silence ensued in the prison cell.

'In retrospect,' he started anew in an increasingly hoarse voice, clearing his throat with difficulty, 'it's perhaps no coincidence that three days ago, just prior to the arrival of Minister

Wu's messenger, I had a knife-fixed note thrown into my hostel room: *A high-flying dragon will have something to regret*. It's a quote from the *Book of Changes*, you know. I was so alarmed that I consulted the classic book for divination, but another sign popped up with a more ominous message: *A hidden dragon should be careful in its movement*. That more than worries me, Xuanji. You know what a dragon can symbolize in our Tang Empire. The dragon symbolism cannot but bring up all its associations to me. I happen to be familiar with the fierce power struggle at the court, and I was terrified by the implication of these signs.'

He saw the terror mirrored in her clear, large eyes. What he had suspected was being confirmed, at least partially, but she was making a visible effort to pull herself together.

'You're a man of great learning, Your Honor. It's no surprise that you're so familiar with classics like the *Book of Changes*. As for those dragon signs or symbols, however, you are just making a mountain out of a molehill. Whatever possible interpretations are involved, how can you be so sure I had a special guest that evening – a guest of the extreme high social status in association with those dragon interpretations? You have nothing whatsoever to prove it.'

Instead of moving further with his second scenario, Judge Dee rose, reached his head out of the cell, and said in a loud voice to Huang and Yang, who were stationed at the end of the corridor, 'You two stand guard there. Don't come over. Don't interrupt our talk. And make sure there is nobody moving near the cell here.'

'Yes,' Yang and Huang said in unison.

'Actually, there is something, Xuanji,' Judge Dee said, turning back to her, 'that goes a long way to prove it. Let me show it to you.'

With a dramatic flourish of his hand, Judge Dee snatched out of the bag the yellow silk underrobe embroidered with golden dragons and spread it out gingerly in front of her.

'Surely you know to whom the yellow underrobe belongs, Xuanji.'

She jumped to her feet, reeled, and then collapsed back to

the heap of straw, her bare back pressing hard against the moss-covered prison wall.

'Where . . . where did you get hold of it?'

'At the crime scene, my assistant Yang found the underrobe wrapped around the waist of Wei – inside his long gown. Wei had taken it out of the nunnery in his flight. It must have seemed valuable to Wei for some reason known only to him.' Judge Dee went on after a theatrical pause, 'Look at the premium silk, at the yellow color, and at the intricate dragon pattern embroidered, and you surely know what it signifies.'

She opened her mouth, yet she ended up saying nothing. Tongue-tied, she averted her eyes while stealing another look at the underrobe.

'A true anecdote may shed a lot of light on the dragon symbolism in question, Xuanji. An early Tang Dynasty general in a southern province had his garden wall ridges decorated with yellow glazed dragons, for which he was impeached as one harboring secret ambition for the throne. As the dragon is known to symbolize imperial power, it's reserved for use only by the emperor – or by the crown prince with some minor modification in the design details. That general managed to save his neck by claiming the dragon decoration on the garden wall had been actually extended from the adjourning Daoist City God Temple, which had a clay statue of the Heavenly Emperor standing majestic in it.

'As for the yellow color, it, too, is commonly known as the "imperial color." People like you and me know better than to wear any clothing of that color. And I don't think you need me to go into details on that.

'Anyway, whoever the owner of the underrobe might have been, he must have been fully aware of its imperial implications. Somehow, he still chose to cling to it.

'So the question we have to ask is: Why?

'And in the light of the yellow silk underrobe, the answer could be staring us in the face. It's because he considered himself entitled to this yellow underrobe embroidered with golden dragons. Consequently, his identity in the scandalous murder case appears to be self-evident, which had to be kept a secret at all costs, and which really accounts for a number of puzzling details of this bizarre case.

'First and foremost, it explains why for some people "high above," the presence of the wearer of the yellow underrobe had to be removed out of any possible scenario of the murder case. The revelation of his involvement in your company – and on that murderous night in the nunnery – could have led to unimaginable, disastrous consequence for the empire. For other people "high above," however, it was an opportunity they could not afford to lose to drag him into the mire—'

'I don't know what you're talking about,' she cut in with a tremulous catch in her voice. 'I'm simply getting more and more befuddled.'

'Well, let's come back to the heart of the matter for the second scenario, Xuanji. Even prior to the murder case, the revelation of his true identity could have lent itself to a number of catastrophic possibilities. One of them would be blackmail, particularly if the man in question happened to be in a vulnerable position. The knowledge of his mixing with someone of your social status would cause him enormous harm. In such a scenario, who could have been the blackmailer?'

Xuanji still made no response, her head hung low, overwhelmed by the unfolding scenario. Judge Dee waited and then resumed in the ensuing silence.

'I don't think you told Wei anything, Xuanji, about the identity of the mysterious man in the yellow underrobe, though you might have asked Wei to prowl around in the black fox spirit costume at night. It was the precaution you wanted to take for that man in the yellow underrobe. As the village folk would be too scared at the sight of the skulking black fox to step into the vicinity of the nunnery, the mysterious movements of the man in the yellow underrobe would not have been noticed, detected by the village people.

'The flower girl, too, was not supposed to know anything about the man in the yellow underrobe, so she was barred from stepping into the nunnery in the last month or so.

'Who else, then, could have had any first-hand knowledge of the clandestine visits by that special guest in the yellow silk underrobe – and of his real identity, too?

'Ning, the one and only maidservant in the nunnery. She practically stayed there with you all the time. Even on the occasions of poetry parties, there're a lot of things for her to do as a maidservant. In some large households, a maidservant has to serve in the bedroom as well – giving a helping hand in the most intimate moments of *cloud turning into rain, and rain turning into cloud*. I don't think she did that, but you would not have kept those visitors – or that special visitor of late – a secret from her. A capable, clever girl, Ning must have learned or guessed something, one way or another, about his real identity. So what could she have possibly done?

'Blackmail. That afternoon, instead of leaving for her home as she had told you, Ning waited at the nunnery, searching for possible evidence and preparing for a showdown with you. She knew he was coming over that night, and that you would try to keep his identity hidden at any cost. Confronted with such an unscrupulous, ungrateful blackmailer, you started cursing, whipping, kicking, and hitting at her hysterically, perhaps not totally aware of how savage, how violent your beating was. In your subconscious mind, you could have chosen to silence her – once and for all – with one involuntary yet fatal blow after another raining on the maidservant . . .

'You did not stop until she dropped to the floor, breathing her last breath.

'And then the man in the silk yellow underrobe did come over – about dinner-time, I assume. Ning was already dead, lying cold on the floor. When you told him what had happened, it was he, not Wei, who helped with the burial of Ning's body in the backyard that night. As a man of high status, he was not used to the digging work, which accounted for the poor, amateur job he did in the backyard.

'But I have to say a good word for that special guest of yours. It was by no means easy for him to take such a huge risk helping you out, though he did so not just for you, but probably more for himself. He could not afford to have his true identity exposed because of it.

'For you, I also have to say something. It was not for yourself that you did all this during the last couple of months – having Wei prowl around in that black fox spirit costume, barring the flower girl from the nunnery, arranging for the printing of the special edition of no more than two copies, doing the exorbitant shopping that morning, and then confronting Ning with the fatal beating . . . It was for him, whose identity you had to keep in absolute secrecy, a man of exceptional noble status, but also one exceptionally vulnerable at the moment.

'That's why in that "confession" of yours, you said not a single word that could possibly incriminate him, even though you knew the statements you made both in the courtroom and in the prison cell were far from convincing. You did not divulge the secret in spite of those cruel tortures you suffered, Xuanji. Truly, you care too much for him.'

Perhaps Judge Dee had intended to conclude the scenario with a romantic touch. He immediately came to regret it, however, with the last sentence fading into the somber silence of the prison cell.

'It's such a long, complicated scenario!' She finally managed to utter the words. 'But all this must have come into your mind like the knife note in the hostel, flashing out of nowhere in the dark, Your Honor.'

'No, it came to me gradually, piece by piece. First, Minister Wu's request for my help in the investigation, which appeared to be more than surprising or suspicious to me. I've long been seen as an obstacle to his ambition for the throne, as you probably know. Why should he have gone out of his way to enlist my help with your case? It was obvious that Minister Wu was desperately after something or someone you have not acknowledged in the confession. Let me repeat: something or someone that justified, in the midst of the black fox spirit skulking here and there in the neighborhood, the killing of the maidservant Ning, of Wei, and of the flower girl Zhang.'

To his astonishment, she then sat up on the heap of straw. She combed her hair with her fingers, drew back her bare legs and feet in a formal position, before she placed the hairy black fox costume across her white thighs. It presented an unbelievably weird sight.

What was the possible meaning of that sudden pose?

A black fox spirit, bestial, demeaned as it was, would still hold on to its dignity, in spite of anything Judge Dee might have chosen to say.

'What happened in the nunnery that day,' she said, having regained her composure, 'I did not exactly remember, Your Honor. I was so drunk. For all I know, there could have been a black fox spirit lurking around, casting a deadly spell. As for the yellow silk underrobe, I know nothing about it. Perhaps Wei alone would be able to tell you how and where he had obtained it. As you have said, the dead take secrets into the grave. For such a bizarre murder case, some people may stubbornly push ahead with all sorts of interpretations or scenarios, but I cannot make up for things that did not happen.'

Judge Dee began wondering whether he had no choice but to take the riskiest gamble in his long official career when a huge dark-gray rat scurried out of nowhere, pattering through the rancid cell floor, producing the same eerie sound as before, and proving something he had suspected earlier.

'As I mentioned earlier,' Judge Dee resumed, appearing to change the subject again, 'I really admire your poems. And I'm serious about the project of compiling a new collection of your poetry. That way, your work will be read not just by those in the circle of poets, but also by a larger group of readers for generations and generations.

'In my research for the project, I met with Mo, the typesetter and publisher of your first poetry collection, and learned about your plan for the new, unheard-of edition of two copies. An edition of no more than two copies did not make any sense, at least as it appears to me, unless it is produced for that man you compared to a soaring dragon in the poem Mo showed me.'

'You have read that poem? It's impossible . . .' she said in a frightened voice.

She did not finish the sentence. Perhaps she was not sure about whether she had left the poem with Mo.

'It's a poem in a different style,' he said, without responding to her question. 'Mo agreed with me that it makes an almost unbelievable departure from your earlier works. It is informed with the high-flying expectations for the future that's unfolding before your eyes.

'Indeed, anything is possible – whether in poetry or in real life. Just think about the early days of our empress, the days before she became the empress, as we both know the part well. If I remember correctly, she also wrote a very moving poem for the man she once cared for. It was a forbidden affair at the time with a huge risk for the lovers if it became known.

'And just between you and me, I would like to touch on another coincidence. She, too, was a Daoist nun at the time she composed the poem. Truly, for a woman with soaring aspirations, only the sky resplendent with the golden, divine dragon could be the limit.'

The way Judge Dee was discussing the case in the prison cell, in the company of Xuanji, if ever reported to the 'people high above,' could have landed him in no end of trouble.

'So I was sort of torn between the two scenarios,' he said, almost losing his voice with his throat so dry. He had been doing most of the talking in the prison cell, not to mention the prolonged discussion with Mayor Pei earlier. 'After all, what about the evidence for the second scenario, as you have asked? You have denied knowledge of the yellow silk underrobe found on Wei's body. True, whatever the secret, he took it into the grave.

'But last night, another poem of yours tipped the scale toward the second scenario.'

'What kind of a poem are you talking about now, Your Honor?'

'Last night, the flower girl Zhang, in whose company you composed the poem "To a Girl in the Neighborhood," delivered to me a new poem you wrote just last month. It's titled "The Fading Peony" – a brand-new piece I have never read or heard about before.'

'Oh, it's nothing but some lines I dashed out at random in the flower garden, where I picked a bouquet of peonies marked for sale. The peonies were perhaps two or three days old, fading a little, but all the more touching.'

'It is a touching poem, full of lofty aspirations that totally become a beautiful, talented poetess like you.'

He stood up, spread the poem out on the stool in front of Xuanji, and sat down on the ground beside her.

The Fading Peony

So many blossoms falling,
falling in the wind, I am sighing,
with the fragrance fading,
failing in the disappearance
of yet another spring.
The peony proves to be too expensive
for the close-fisted customers,
and its sweet scent, too strong
for the flirting butterflies.
The royal palace alone deserves
such a blaze of red petals.
How can the green foliage
endure the dust and dirt
by the roadside?
Only with its transplantation
into the grand imperial garden
will those young dandies
come to regret.

'It's in your elegant handwriting, no question about it. I happened to have with me a scroll of another poem in your own calligraphy – "To a Girl in the Neighborhood," which you "copied out for Wei as well."' He produced the scroll out of the bag before he added emphatically, stroking his beard, 'So evidently.'

She stared at him, ripples of fear reflecting in her eyes.

'It's a common practice for poets and poetesses to write about flowers or trees to project their own feelings, whether in terms of symbolism or objective correlative. In this piece, you compare yourself to the unappreciated peony – too expensive for those cheap customers, and too strongly fragrant for the flirting butterflies. The image of its enduring "dust and dirt by the roadside" makes a vivid description of the life, as you see it, in the midst of those depraved parties in the nunnery. But what more than shocks me is the extended metaphor of transplanting the peony into the royal garden. It's such a daring figure of speech. So you're moving out – into the imperial garden, which is metonymy here, mind you. In other words, you're moving into the company of the man whose very home is the royal palace of the Tang Empire. When that happens, those short-sighted, cold-hearted dandies who have not appreciated you will surely come to regret it.

'In short, the poem showed a so-far-unseen side of you – a secret side, and an ambitious side.'

'Peony is just a metaphor in the poem,' she said, without looking up to meet his eyes. 'You know better than to make such a far-fetched interpretation of it.'

'You don't have to worry about my interpretation. I'm a big fan of your poetry. But what about the interpretations made by others? You must have heard of the political debate about the peony being named the national flower. Her Majesty is adamantly against it, as her new empire needs to name a different national flower. And you write not only about the peony, but in association with the royal palace as well. Absolutely a matter of political crime. The barely educated flower girl might not have grasped the political implication of the poem, but people like Minister Wu will not miss it for anything.'

'So you're going to show this poem to Minister Wu?'

'I don't think too highly of Minister Wu, as you probably know. Nor am I a judge officially assigned to the case. But I'm under a lot of pressure from Minister Wu and others.

'So I have to be frank with you, Xuanji. As long as your account fails to convince others, and the case drags on like that with more and more collateral damage for reasons known only to those at the very top, Mayor Pei and those people high above will have to bring pressure to bear upon you with the ongoing investigation and interrogation, and the horrible tortures in prison as well. Soon another trial, and then still another. All the possible aspects of the case will be examined and re-examined.

'As for me, Minister Wu wants me to look into your case with a special authorization letter, which has probably been approved by Her Majesty. Without any breakthrough, I think I have to tell him what research I have done, and what possible evidence I have found. For instance, the yellow silk underrobe was discovered on Wei's body, so there's probably no withholding it. And then the black fox spirit costume. And the peony poem, too. For a celebrated poetess like you, it's natural for people to study your poems for all the imaginable clues. If I could succeed in getting hold of "The Fading Peony," it's only a matter of time before others do so, too.

'Eventually, the mysterious guest in the yellow silk underrobe who came to the nunnery that evening will also be discovered and dragged into the mire. It's not inconceivable.

'So let me repeat it just one more time, Xuanji: the investigation will have to continue the way I have just described, I am afraid, unless you come up with a more convincing confession. A more acceptable one, if you know what I mean.'

Instead of making an immediate response, Xuanji seemed to be tucking the black fox spirit costume tight around her hardly covered groin, as if she had been reincarnated through the posture.

It was absurd of him to think so, he knew. A weird, ominous shroud of silence reigned over the darksome prison cell.

'I'm overwhelmed, Your Honor,' she finally said, biting her lower lip so hard that it started bleeding. 'But you're an honest and capable judge of the Tang Empire. You surely can do something about the case, can't you?'

'I don't know about that. The way Minister Wu brought me into the case, as it seems to my assistant Yang, could be a devious trap. Not just for me, but for who Minister Wu believes is the one involved in it – in the yellow dragon-embroidered underrobe – in the background. You are an intelligent woman, Xuanji, I believe you know I don't have to say more.'

What cannot be said has to be passed over in silence.

'And I don't think I'm cut out for a judge's role anymore. I've not spent a very long while talking to you here in the cell, but I already feel worn out; my tongue is dry and I'm losing my voice. I'm getting too old.'

She looked puzzled by his abrupt shift to self-pity.

'So I have to go out for a cup of hot tea, and I'll bring a cup back for you. You need to have a short break, too, Xuanji. In the meantime, you may think about what I've just discussed with you – about the dire consequence for the continuation of the investigation and interrogation.'

He rose, stretched his legs, and made his exit shakily as Xuanji remained in nonplused silence.

Again, it took a while before Judge Dee carried a pot of fresh hot tea back into the cell. She was sitting still with her back against the sordid wall, her head hung low, her face even paler than before, half covered by the long black hair.

'Have a cup of fresh hot tea, Xuanji.'

She took the cup of tea he had poured out for her, but she placed it on the floor, and without taking a sip, she sat up straight and said, 'Why people call you Judge Dee, I think I now can really understand. So ingenious, so honest, and so infallible. What you have said about Wei is vividly true, as if you yourself had witnessed everything from the very beginning.'

He waited for her to go on, without trying to make any comment in response as she lightly touched the black fox costume again.

'About Wei, I think I can guess why he had the black fox costume made for himself in secret. From time to time, he came to my place at night – you know that. In fact, I might have said something to him about the neighbors pointing fingers at his back, and cursing like a bunch of self-righteous moralists. It was unpleasant, to say the least, to both me and Wei. He wanted to scare them away. He had said to me more than once that he did not want those prying neighbors to cause me any trouble.

'Wei's a good-for-nothing man – I knew that long ago – but it was not that easy for him to stay on with my fiery temperament. And to give the devil his due, he cared for me in his way. His wearing the black fox spirit costume proved it. I'm an ill-starred woman, and I'm finished. I knew that only too well in the courtroom. I did not mention him in the statement because, after all, it was he – not the other people – who helped me with the burial job in the backyard despite the fact that I killed Ning, a younger slut who had just slept with him. So why should I have dragged him into the mire because of me?

'Now he's dead, I don't think I have to worry about it anymore, and I will make a truthful confession, however hard and humiliating for me, to admit my relationship with an unworthy man like Wei, and to admit killing my maidservant Ning out of a fit of insane jealousy.'

She was literally taking over the first scenario Judge Dee had represented to her without saying one single word about the validity of the second, though she mentioned that 'he – not the other people' helped with the burial job in an implied negation of the presence of the special guest in the yellow silk underrobe. She was a clever one.

To his consternation, she then re-combed her hair with her fingers, wetted her cracked lips with her tongue, edged down from the heap of straw, knelt in front of him, and slowly unfastened the belt of her wrap.

With the wrap falling down from her body, she prostrated her naked self at his feet.

It presented a shocking, surreal scene.

Despite having washed herself earlier, her naked back was smeared greenish again through contact with the moss-covered cell wall, and a layer of loose straw was stuck to her bare, bruised buttocks.

The posture kept the front of her body partially out of sight, but he could not help glimpsing her white breasts flattened hard against the cold cell floor.

It was not a gesture to show her gratitude, nor likely an attempt to seduce him. In those glamorous nights of her fashionable poetry parties, ironically, such a dramatic tableau could have overwhelmed a bookish old man like Judge Dee. But not here, not at this moment, not with her torture-ravaged, cell-sullied body groveling in the dust.

What was the point of her choosing to make such a degrading gesture at this moment?

He was struck with a vague, inexplicable, uneasy sense of déjà vu. Somewhere he might have seen or read about the strange pose, but for the moment, the meaning of her prostration at his feet eluded him.

'I'm putting myself at your mercy, Your Honor. There is no point having the case drag on like this; you're surely right about it. I have suffered more than enough in prison. With this truthful confession, you may put an end to the investigation.'

So it was a gesture begging for mercy – but why should she have made it in such a self-humiliating way?

In a shaft of light penetrating through the rusted iron bars of the cell, his glance fell on the shining yellow silk underrobe beside her on the ground, and he saw her clutching its sleeve – perhaps subconsciously – in her trembling hand.

He felt his heart sinking at the connection of it.

What had been worrying him from the beginning turned out to be true. The posture on her part made a subtle yet unmistakable acknowledgment of the identity of the man she had been seeing in the yellow silk underrobe.

She did not have to say his name – Prince Li, her secret lover from the Tang royal family.

To those Li loyalists, the crown prince was entitled to such a piece of imperial clothing with dragons embroidered on it. Prince Li himself must have believed it, too.

So Xuanji's pose came like an echo from a fallen empire in the ancient time. Judge Dee was hit with the recollection of it – a defeated king, along with his queen and imperial concubines, surrendered themselves to the conqueror outside the surrounded city, kneeling with their bodies stripped naked to the waist, groveling in utter submission in the dust.

For the present moment, Xuanji was literally imagining herself into the one beside the prince, begging for mercy nakedly like a queen, or an imperial concubine, with the same pose, even though the prince was not there, prostrating himself alongside her in the dust.

To his consternation, Judge Dee became disoriented at the sight of something like a fly stuck on her white bare sole – or merely a smudge in spite of the wash she had taken in the cell. He was getting too old, he thought.

'You are known as one of the most loyal, capable Confucianist officials of the Great Tang Empire, Your Honor. But for you, the country could have been irreparably ruined by unscrupulous conspirators like Minister Wu under Her Majesty. I'm so grateful for what you have been doing for the empire all these years. And this time, like other times, you'll do the right thing for the Great Tang Empire, I believe.'

The message for mercy became even clearer. The degrading

posture was made, not for herself, but for the prince.

For the Great Tang Empire of the Li family.

She was begging Judge Dee not to have the prince implicated in the conclusion of the case.

That night, it was the prince, not Wei, who came to the nunnery, and who had helped with the burial in the backyard.

The way the investigation was going, it would most likely be a matter of time for people to trace it to the prince, as Judge Dee had supposed.

Even the role of an accomplice could turn out to be too much trouble for the prince, who had been recently exiled from the capital. Were it to be found that the prince, instead of staying out of the capital as ordered by the empress, had become involved with a notorious courtesan in the nunnery on the outskirts of Chang'an – possibly a reminder of the empress in her younger days in a Daoist nunnery – the disastrous consequences could be easily imagined.

But it was not the moment for Judge Dee to think too much about all this, with Xuanji still groveling and kowtowing in the dust at his feet.

'Please get up, Xuanji. I do not have the final say in this case, as you know, but I'll try my best to do the right thing, I give you my word,' he promised vaguely, though he could not help wondering what the right thing could possibly be, and how he could possibly do it.

'I totally understand, Your Honor. In your first scenario, your analysis of the murder case is really thorough and well founded about Wei's affair with the maid, about my fit of insane jealousy that led to her death, about Wei's help with the burial job that night, and about my initial unwillingness to make a clean breast of it. Finally, you have helped me see the light. I have no other choice, I know, but to sign a new, truthful confession to the murder.'

'If you want to make a new statement – a more admissible one with all the convincing details, you need to talk to Mayor Pei. And I think you can give him the black fox spirit costume. That may explain a lot of the inscrutable things in the case. Of course, I'll talk to Mayor Pei, and perhaps to Minister Wu, too, and they, anxious for a speedy conclusion of a high-profile case, may be willing to listen to me.'

'Thank you so much. And I know what I shall say to Mayor Pei.'

'As for the peony poem, Xuanji, it may not be too good an idea for me to put in this edition of your poetry collection, but perhaps later, in a revised edition.' He then rose, putting into his own bag the piece of paper with the peony poem written on it, the yellow silk dragon-embroidered underrobe, and the scroll of Xuanji's calligraphy.

It was an unmistakable hint that he would not give them to others, provided Xuanji held on to the scenario she had given him.

'I really appreciate it. I know how much I owe you for the speedy conclusion of the case. Oh, Judge Dee – can I call you Judge Dee?'

Emerging out of the prison cell, Judge Dee felt another wave of weariness – closer to sickness – washing over him.

Huang, the prison guard, was hurrying over, carrying a tray of wok-fried sticky rice snacks in his hands, and looking up at Judge Dee with a ludicrous, obsequious grin.

Judge Dee decided not to go back to Mayor Pei. He did not know what he could tell Pei. Xuanji would have to tell Pei first, and then Judge Dee would corroborate Xuanji's version, adding his comments like a poetry collection compiler. The 'new confession' would, he hoped, not differ too much from the first scenario he had described to her inside the prison cell.

On the spur of the moment, he dashed off a couple of lines on a scrap of paper.

She's willing to talk to you now, I think. Wei was connected, but not the flower girl Zhang. I have to start preparing for my trip early tomorrow morning.

It was not his case. There was no point Judge Dee putting his finger into Mayor Pei's pie. Whatever the outcome now, it would not be his problem, nor would he want to take any credit.

Nor was it a matter of his being too modest for the possible 'breakthrough.' On the contrary, it would not do him any good to get caught in the cobweb of all the dirty, high-stake politics behind the murder case.

He wondered whether Mayor Pei might have already reported to Minister Wu about his visit to Xuanji in prison, but he did not really care.

'Give this to Mayor Pei, Huang. Send for a doctor to check on her. And a tailor, too. Here is a small piece of silver. All the expense on me.'

'Whatever you order, Your Excellency,' the prison guard responded with another bow.

'And send in the tray of snacks to her first.'

The air outside was unexpectedly refreshing, but Judge Dee found himself submerged in depression, devoid of any excitement at the likely conclusion of the case.

'Any breakthrough?' Yang raised the question to his master the moment Huang hurried out of sight, heading back to the cell.

'I don't know, but I think she may start talking. By the way, your discovery of the black fox spirit costume helped tremendously. Wei wore that for his nocturnal visits to her in the nunnery.'

'That's unbelievable, but finally we may be able to put the story of the black fox spirit to rest.'

'Well, I don't know about that, either.'

What she had said about Wei inside the prison cell was only partially true. As an accomplice in the murder, there would be no end of speculation about the reason for his wearing the black fox costume to scare away the neighbors in the depth of the dark night.

All in all, Judge Dee was not too sure whether Xuanji's revised statement would prove to be that acceptable to Mayor Pei, Minister Wu, and the 'people above,' but a 'speedy conclusion' would appear to be in the interests of the Great Tang Empire. They all knew that.

It started to drizzle again in an enveloping mist.

That night, back in his room at the temple, Judge Dee began writing a letter to Minister Wu.

He began by highlighting his investigation-through-poetry approach, mentioning his plan for a possible collection of

Xuanji's poetry, and his visit to the prison as an integrated part of it, though he refrained from saying anything about the yellow silk underrobe and the peony poem. The visit to the prison confirmed, among other things, Wei being the 'true-hearted lover' in the poem 'To a Girl in the Neighborhood.' From that, he came up with the hypothesis that Xuanji's motive in the murder case was insane jealousy, as was understandable for a woman devastated by too many betrayals in her life. Wei's amorous tryst with Ning became the last straw for Xuanji, and in a murderous breakdown, she savagely beat the maid to death. And because of it, Wei later turned into an accomplice in the backyard burial. Judge Dee did not go into detail about the scenario, leaving it largely blank as in a traditional Chinese landscape painting for the viewer's imagination. Minister Wu should be able to get most of it. Judge Dee merely added that after his talk with her in the prison, Xuanji seemed to have acquiesced with his analysis.

As for Wei's death, Judge Dee did not think it was very important to Minister Wu or Mayor Pei. So he touched on a couple of related hypothetical points in passing: Wei's wearing the black fox spirit costume struck terror into the neighborhood, so he was able to visit Xuanji at night without worrying about being seen by the neighbors, and Xuanji's mentioning him as an impossible womanizer who paid the price in the end. Judge Dee did not even mention the death of the flower girl, Zhang. It could have been unrelated to the Xuanji case. Nothing but a coincidence. And he did not think Mayor Pei would have mentioned the killing near the temple in connection, which would not be a credit to the mayor.

'Of course, there may be some other details not yet covered in the scenario about the Xuanji case. It is such a complicated, sensational case, and it's definitely in the interests of the Great Tang Empire for us to have a speedy and acceptable conclusion, as you have said to me. Being so pressed for time, however, I can give you only a case report based on my investigation done during the last three days. Tomorrow morning, I have to leave for the new post entrusted to me by Her Majesty, as you know.'

Putting down the brush pen, he thought he'd better say

something more, but he found himself dried up like the dried ink stone staring up at him, black, cold, hard.

The black tea leaves rising and sinking suspiciously in the cup, he took another sip of the lukewarm tea. And he noted a thin cracked line cutting across the surface of the ink stone, which could soon become too damaged for use.

It was a quiet, peaceful night in the temple. In the distance, however, someone was heard playing a pensive melody on a bamboo flute.

A stanza of a *ci* poem floated across his mind, as if flowing out of the flute melody under the dark night.

The flute sobbing,
waking from her dream,
she sees the moon shining,
above the high tower. The moon
shining above the high tower,
the willows turn green again, year
after year, along Baling Bridge,
where lovers sadly part.

The authorship of the *ci* poem remained unknown, but it had recently been circulated a lot in connection to the Xuanji case. Some scholars claimed that it was her poem. Judge Dee also felt rather inclined to include it in the collection of Xuanji's poems, if he ever managed to compile it one of these days.

Without worrying too much about the authorship, the sensibility of the poem could have truly applied to Xuanji. She was waiting for her man, year after year, but to no avail. 'Baling Bridge' in the first stanza referred to a scenic location in the capital where lovers would choose to part, with the verdant willows weeping in the background. She, too, could have been standing there, holding on to the willow shoot, as if gazing out of the willow poem she had once written in the company of Wen, which had made her name widely known in the circle of poets.

Judge Dee could not exactly recall the second stanza of the poem, which seemed to be shifting to a more impersonal tone, with the introduction of the image of a 'royal mausoleum' lifting the poem to an everlasting sadness at a universal level, yet also carrying an ominous note about her tragic life, waiting for Wen, for Zi'an, without seeing a messenger bringing the message so crucial to her, and then toward the end of her life, waiting, waiting for the man in the yellow silk dragon-embroidered underrobe, with the moon shining on the high tower – no, into the dark prison cell, still no message coming along the ancient path.

Once again, Judge Dee wished he too could write a poem like hers, but he had reached an age, he told himself, when he could admit what was beyond him. So many years he had wasted playing politics, which, unlike poetry, would not survive him.

FIVE

After a short, broken sleep, Judge Dee rose in the early morning with the rain pattering against the lattice window, as if pattering in a half-forgotten dream.

In the temple courtyard, a sleepy-eyed, palm-leaf-capped-and-clad monk was yawning, stretching himself, and then beginning to strike the large bronze bell for the morning service, blow after blow, the sound reverberating into the impenetrable mist and rain.

It was time for Judge Dee to check out, he knew. Yang was waiting outside his room, ready to resume the journey with his master.

The white-browed abbot Stainless, Nameless, and a bevy of other senior monks immediately came out of the black-painted gate to see them off.

It was perhaps too early for Han Shan, who was also a guest in the temple, but then Judge Dee saw the poet monk hurrying over with a silk scroll in his hand.

'The temple actually has a batch of ready-made blank scrolls for visitors like us. So I've just copied out a new poem of mine for you. After our talk about Xuanji's poetry the day before yesterday, I had a sudden impulse for these lines.'

So Han Shan and Judge Dee unfurled the scroll between themselves, with each holding on to one end of it. On the rice-white paper was a poem written in vigorous brush pen calligraphy. Dee started reading it aloud with those monks standing around, nodding and murmuring in approval.

'The stars spreading out, far and wide,
present a deeper, sincerer night sky.
Refusing to sink, the moon
hangs on like a solitary light burning
against the steep mountain cliff.

No need for any polishing,
the moon appears so round, bright:
suspending still in the night sky
is my very heart.'

Judge Dee then noticed a line in small characters to the left bottom of the scroll: *After talking with Judge Dee about Xuanji's poems in the temple.*

'Thank you so much, Han Shan. I really appreciate it. What a marvelous Zen poem! The bright moon is your heart, and your heart is the bright moon. No difference between the subject and the object. The last couple of lines that "*suspending still in the night sky / is my very heart*" speaks volumes about your unwavering spirit.'

'Well, you're an unwavering judge, Dee, a man for doing things in the world of red dust,' Han Shan said, smiling, producing a copy of a time-yellowed booklet out of his ample sleeve. 'Still, a Buddhist classic like *Diamond Sutra* may turn out to be helpful to you when you find yourself lost in the confusion between appearance and reality. So here is an old copy handwritten by Xuanzang for you.'

'Xuanzang, the master who has come back from pilgrimage to the west with all these scriptures! It's extremely valuable! I cannot thank you enough, Han Shan.'

Judge Dee bid his farewell to Han Shan, the abbot, Nameless, and the other monks standing and waving their hands on the stone steps.

Outside, the new willow shoots appeared green, glistening with the morning rain. The scene reminded Judge Dee again of the melancholy willow poem composed by Xuanji when she first met Wen. In spite of the success of the poem at the time, a critic commented that the sentiment of the poem did not bode well for the future of the young girl. Dee was depressed at the thought of it. Poetry could foretell.

Yang followed his master in dogged silence, as if Judge Dee's mood had somehow proved to be contagious. It was not too surprising a decision for them to leave the temple that morning, but it took Yang quite a while to have the carriage set up for the long trip.

Before getting into the carriage, Judge Dee looked over his shoulder again. A solitary old dog loitered out into a patch of the shade near the temple gate, staring up as if in wonder at the hustle and bustle of the travelers in the mundane world. A curl of smoke rose in leisure from the red and gray roofs scattered at the foot of the hills. The morning seemed to present a peaceful panorama that the morning itself did not understand.

'You may take a short nap in the carriage, Master. The candlelight in your room kept on flickering long after midnight, I noticed. You have to take good care of yourself. After all, Xuanji's is not our case. You have done everything possible about it, but there's only so much you can do. In the meantime, there's such a lot of work waiting for you at the new post.'

Judge Dee, too, tried to tell himself that he had done all he possibly could have for the Xuanji case, but he decided not to say anything to Yang about his talk with Xuanji in the prison cell the day before.

Nor about the possible result of it, which Judge Dee himself did not yet know.

But it was time to get ready for the new job as an imperial circuit supervisor, even though he found himself not in any mood for it. He had had a bad taste in his mouth when he woke up, and he still failed to get rid of the lingering tang.

Hardly had Judge Dee squeezed himself inside the carriage, pulling down the curtain and half-closing his eyes, when he heard a horse galloping over from the ancient path in front of the temple and to a sudden stop by the carriage.

He lifted up the curtain in a hurry.

It was a messenger from Mayor Pei, a black-attired man dismounting from the horse, still panting breathlessly from the ride over at full speed.

'His Excellency wanted me to hurry over and give this letter to you before you leave.'

Taking the envelope, Judge Dee said, 'Tell Mayor Pei that I will read the letter during the journey.'

Sitting in the front, Yang appeared to be shaking his head in silent resignation and cracking his whip loudly. It would be useless, he knew, to try to dissuade Judge Dee from reading the letter instead of taking a much-needed nap in the carriage.

Judge Dee pulled out the letter, as he had promised the messenger, the moment the carriage started rolling along the bumpy road.

After the usual, official pleasantries at the beginning, the letter recaptured the main points of the talk between Xuanji and Mayor Pei the previous day, which had happened shortly after Judge Dee left the prison.

In a nutshell, she made a new, different statement about the murder case. In accordance with this latest version, she killed Ning not in a drunken blackout but in a jealous rage because that afternoon, when she got back from her shopping, she discovered the affair between Ning and Wei in the nunnery.

For a fairly long time, Xuanji had been crazy about Wei, calling him 'a true-hearted lover' in a poem written in the days when the two of them had first met. She believed him to be one capable of playing fine tunes for her poems, saying all the sweet words to her ears, and pledging fidelity to her, not to mention his proving to be a tireless stud in bed. He was poor, but with those 'visitors' of hers lavishing gifts and money on her, she was in a position to help him out financially. It was not just men who were capable of buying things for a woman like her; she, too, had the satisfaction of being able to take care of a man like Wei, purchasing all sorts of things for him, including the hut close to the nunnery. Later on, she was disappointed with the discovery that Wei received favors and money from other women as well, but she found herself already addicted to him, physically, if not metaphysically, as in those lines she had composed for him in the moment of their rolling about in clouds and rain in bed. As long as he declared his fidelity to her face, she acquiesced. After all, she, too, had been seeing other men all the time.

But on that eventful second day of the month, Xuanji was in for a devastating surprise. With the maidservant Ning scheduled to leave in the morning, Xuanji went out shopping by herself. Upon her return to the nunnery, however, she was shocked to see Ning still there, running out barefoot, her face flushed and her hair disheveled. What's more, she saw that a man's hat – Wei's – was left on the mahogany chair. When she confronted Ning, the latter mumbled that Wei had come and gone, unable to explain why she had not left as scheduled in the morning. Then Xuanji stepped into the bedroom to a more shocking scene of a pillow thrown on the floor, of a wet patch on the bedsheet, and of a pubic hair curled up on the rumpled bed, which Xuanji remembered having made herself in the morning.

It dawned on her that Wei must have arrived before Ning's departure, had a 'quickie' with her, and fled upon Xuanji's return in such a hurry – with no time even to clean up the mess in the bedroom, or to retrieve the hat left on the chair.

That discovery proved to be too much for Xuanji, who was crushed with the humiliation of having lost Wei to a maid in her service. Flying into a blinding rage, she started beating, whipping, and kicking Ning with all her strength. In fact, she was not really aware of what she was doing in the hysterical fit – until it was too late. Ning dropped dead, all of a sudden, with a thud on the floor of the bedroom.

Shortly afterward, Wei came over to the nunnery again – to the shocking scene of Ning's body lying cold there. He managed to calm Xuanji down and hurried out to dig a shallow hole in the backyard, as if doing some tree-planting yardwork. Later on, under the cover of the black night, he and Xuanji carried out the body of Ning and buried her in the hole.

But they were too nervous to do a proper job in the backyard, so Ning's bloody body began to smell from under a thin layer of soil and attracted the flies over the next day, a scene that appeared too suspicious to the guests there, who immediately reported it to the local authorities.

Xuanji had not confessed in the courtroom because it was too humiliating for her to acknowledge, so it seemed to her, that a celebrated, beautiful poetess could have lost her man to a humble maid like Ning.

Magistrate Pei and Xuanji then also discussed the death of

Wei. It seemed to Xuanji, after she was thrown into prison with the mounting pressure brought to bear upon her, that Wei must have become panic-stricken. He thought it would only be a matter of time before she cracked and gave him up. So he decided to take flight after scooping up the valuables in Xuanji's bedroom into a large bundle, but he could have been seen sneaking out of the nunnery with the bundle on his back. Someone in the neighborhood – possibly a villager – must have noticed his furtive movements and come up with the mugging plan. And that's how Wei ended up being mugged and killed on the road in front of the nunnery.

As for the flower girl's death, Xuanji said she did not know anything about it. It happened late at night, with hardly any people moving around, so the mayor seemed to believe that it was done by a local criminal. The flower girl was a 'bit coquettish,' according to some of the villagers, and it was possibly a sex crime that happened at night. The examination done at the crime scene later also fitted with the scenario, though no one could really tell why the flower girl was there. In appearance, it was unrelated to Xuanji's case, and Mayor Pei saw no point connecting it with the other deaths. Particularly for a nobody like the flower girl, it made sense for the death not to be considered as part of Xuanji's case. Any further complication would not have been in the interests of the mayor.

'I don't know how I can ever thank you enough, Judge Dee,' Mayor Pei concluded in sincerity. 'It's a very convincing confession, I have to say, particularly about her motive. After so many cruel letdowns in her life, the betrayal by Wei and Ning became the last straw for her. She killed the maidservant in an uncontrollable rage that afternoon. As for the burial of the body in the backyard, it's no longer something unimaginable with Wei acting as her accomplice in the night. She said repeatedly she had not told the truth because it was too mortifying for her to admit such a defeat to a low-life maidservant like Ning; and because she still cared for Wei in her way, she tried hard not to drag him into the trouble. However, his death changed everything.

'All in all, it's a believable statement, acceptable with so many bizarre details in the case convincingly explained. I don't think those men of letters or any other busybodies could have anything else to say about the conclusion.'

So the latest version – the one in the letter grasped in his hand – was pretty much the first scenario Judge Dee had suggested to her in the prison cell, with Xuanji represented as a murderer driven by jealousy, and with Wei cast as an accomplice, though it was not without some minor, intriguing modifications here and there improvised by the poetess.

Was that statement a truthful one?

After all, anything was possible for a woman madly in love. At least it could prove to be acceptable to Mayor Pei who was so desperate for a satisfactory conclusion.

But was it possible that her statement was given simply to cover the second scenario involving the man in the yellow silk underrobe embroidered with golden dragons?

When he put the letter back into the envelope, Judge Dee found in it an additional note on a scrap of paper, which Mayor Pei must have added in a hurry in the morning.

'Late last night, I had a talk with Minister Wu. He did not say much about the conclusion, but he mentioned that the empress is also very anxious for a quick conclusion to Xuanji's case. Speculation about the murder case was spreading like wildfire, with all the sordid details imaginable. Her Majesty did not think that it could turn into anything of positive energy for the maintenance of the social stability of the Tang Empire. So the earlier the conclusion, the better for all concerned. An approval for the execution of Xuanji would be quickly made.

'She could be executed as early as today.'

So that was the end.

Judge Dee nodded over the note, stroking his graying beard in a gust of wind.

After all, people saw a murder case, like anything and everything else in the world of red dust, from their own perspective. And, whether consciously or not, in the light of their own interests, too.

For Empress Wu, the political stability of the Tang Empire was the top priority, particularly at a time when people were complaining about the traditional social hierarchy being turned upside down with her – a woman of dubious background similar to Xuanji's – now sitting on the throne. Talk about the Xuanji case with all its spicy details spelled a negative criticism of the current regime, adding fuel to the fire. A quick execution of the poetess with an acceptable, convincing conclusion would therefore prove to be in the interests of the empire, whether she was truly guilty as charged or not.

Internal Minister Wu might not have been too pleased with such an outcome as he failed to obtain anything from Xuanji's latest confession that would incriminate Prince Li, but Wu was in no position to argue with the empress, for he had nothing concrete to support the scenario casting the prince as an accomplice to murder. Still, with both Judge Dee and the prince driven out of the capital for the time being, Minister Wu would have more opportunities for the materialization of his ambitious plan. So the conclusion turned out to be not that unacceptable for the moment.

As for Xuanji, was such an ending acceptable – at least more acceptable than others?

Because of her ultimate sacrifice – at least so she could have imagined – Prince Li remained undiscovered and untouched. For her, that was the best thing that had ever happened to her in her sad, short life. She believed that the prince cared for her, so much so that he took the risk to visit her in the nunnery, and to help her out with the burial in the backyard that night. It was simply overwhelming for her to finally find such a 'true-hearted lover' in the prince.

She sacrificed herself, not just for him but also for the Tang Empire. It was the 'right thing,' as she had told Judge Dee in the prison cell, for her to do – to protect the prince, and to ensure the continuation of the Lis on the throne of the Tang Empire – even at the expense of her life.

For her, there seemed to be meaning in the loss of herself. It was understandable for a poetess who had been searching for 'meaning' all her life.

But was the prince really such a 'true-hearted lover'?

Not too long before his meeting with Xuanji, Judge Dee recalled, the prince had landed himself in trouble for an affair with a palace lady.

To say the least, the prince then made no effort to help Xuanji in prison.

No effort whatsoever to visit her or even send her anything.

After all, it would have been seen as unacceptable for the prince to get involved with a disreputable courtesan like Xuanji, let alone to cast his lot with her.

Consequently, a total erasure of the relationship between the courtesan poetess and the prince was the order of the day. No traces of it should have been left detectable under the Tang Dynasty sun.

Hence the fatal ambush by the black-attired horseman on the road so close to the nunnery. It was to recover anything potentially incriminating the prince that might have been left behind in the nunnery.

Regarding the murder of Wei, it was not likely the prince had directly given the order, but it was far more likely that the people under him had done so – with the prince's tacit approval. As for the message with the stab wound at Wei's groin, it could have been done deliberately as a sort of camouflage, but there might also have been another distorted rationalization for it: whatever Xuanji had been, she was one that had been touched by the prince, and, consequently, was untouchable to others. And of course the black-attired horseman could have been sent by Minister Wu for a different purpose.

And such an ending for Wei was acceptable to the people who were aware, or not, of the conspiracies revolving around the nunnery, in which Wei unwittingly played a shadowy role in his way, wearing the black fox spirit costume in the neighborhood at night, or carrying the cloth bundle out of the nunnery on the last morning of his life. He was nobody. A good-for-nothing nobody missed by no one.

Judge Dee was not so sure about the flower girl, though. She was innocent, and so young. But as an old saying goes, *the fire around the city gate means the death for the fish in a pond at quite a distance, too*. People have to put out the fire by draining out the pond water, harmless as the fish there might be. So the young girl came to an untimely end. Things like that happened; it was nothing new or strange to Judge Dee.

Ironic as it might appear, such a conclusion was also quite acceptable to Judge Dee, he thought, with another wave of unpleasant taste in his mouth. To begin with, he had made an excellent show of the investigation to Minister Wu, who could no longer find any fault with him. On the other hand, Xuanji expressed her heartfelt gratitude to the judge for the 'investigation' into her case. It's the least he could do for the poetess, whose poems he really liked.

And as a Confucianist, Judge Dee did the 'right thing' for the Tang Empire as well.

After all, there are things a judge can do, and things a judge cannot do. It came like an echo redolent of a Confucian maxim his late father had taught him.

There were questions he could not avoid asking himself, though. For one, what had he, the celebrated Judge Dee, really done for Xuanji?

Or was there nothing he had really done for her?

Out of the blue, the flying-knife note flashed back to his mind: '*A high-flying dragon will have something to regret!*' The particular hexagram in the *Book of Changes*, when used as a sign in fortune telling, means that *for the people in high positions with soaring ambitions, they could suffer a turn of luck and have something to regret.* It could have come as a warning from the divine yet inscrutable providence for Judge Dee to behave himself. And for the prince, too. And then the next sign – '*A hidden dragon should be careful in its movement*' – perhaps more explicit as a warning, meaning '*at this stage, it's too early for the dragon to move, so it won't hurt to stay put.*' For him as well as for the prince? Ultimately, it had a bearing on the fate of the Tang Empire . . .

Judge Dee was getting confused again. A Confucianist, he did not believe in supernatural phenomena, but the *Book of Changes* had been considered as a Confucian classic, and those recurring dragon signs, along with intricate images or patterns in the last couple of days, had proven to be so penetrating into the opaqueness of nemesis.

Perhaps there were more things than were dreamed of by a bookish man like the so-called Judge Dee, particularly with his brain worn out as old age approached.

And he was suddenly disgusted with the role he had played in the murder investigation. In reality, he could hardly tell what a role it exactly was. As a Confucian scholar-turned-official in the Tang Empire, he had studied nothing but Confucian classics for the civil service examination, and then as an official because of his success in the examination, he had only the vaguest ideas about being fair, just, or independent when engaged in an investigation like a judge in the shadow of the empire.

As in the Xuanji case, he wished he could have served as nothing but an independent judge, pure and simple. But that was not possible in the Great Tang Empire. The way he became involved in the investigation was nothing but politics. It was out of the question for a Confucianist official like him to contemplate the possibility of causing the prince any irreparable damage, or the possibility of hurting the interests of the Tang Empire. In fact, he had ruled out the idea from the very beginning. Politics had to be placed above law.

That was how he had come to suggest to Xuanji a scenario – the first scenario – which did not appear that convincing even to himself. It turned out to be the very scenario that served as the working basis, nevertheless, for the acceptable conclusion of the murder case to be made.

What's more, Xuanji herself embraced the scenario, even though she was to be put on the scaffold because of it.

She was going to be executed anyway, however, as she could have rationalized the ending for herself with the cold comfort that she did something truly worthy for the prince, and for the Tang Empire as well.

And Judge Dee, too, could justify his work with the fact that the ending, whether he had suggested the scenario or not, would be the same for her.

Then, why not the ending that would have seemed more acceptable than any other to the romantic poetess in the dark, damp prison cell?

The curtain was falling for her, the order of the acts
predetermined in the shadow of the Empire . . .

The two lines came out of nowhere in the suffocating carriage. He tried to produce a couple of lines more for a poem while pondering on Xuanji's tragic fate, and on his ignoble compromise made between politics and justice, but the futile effort began to wear him out.

He would never be able to write poems like Xuanji; that much he had been sure of.

And it was also true, as Yang had observed, that he had slept so little last night. It would be a long, daunting, difficult journey stretching out ahead of him, whether he wanted to think about it or not.

His heavy eyelids closing in spite of himself, Judge Dee thought he might be able to doze off for a short while in the carriage.

And the monotonous ride on the bumpy road eventually lent itself to a wave of drowsiness, which appeared to be more than acceptable to him.

Much to his annoyance, a blue-headed fly was bumping in the carriage, buzzing, flipping, humming, and circling stubbornly around his head.

The carriage space was small, suffocating. He pulled up the curtain and waved his hand about forcefully. The droning ceased. The moment the curtain fell back down, however, the monotonous noise returned.

He felt terribly bugged.

'You don't recognize me, do you?' the fly flew over and whispered in a sweet, seductive voice. 'I was the one that kept licking her bare sole in that dark prison cell. You stared long and hard at me, I knew.'

'No, I thought it was a small smudge at the arch of her foot.'

He recalled gazing at her bare feet, smooth and shapely, in sharp contrast to the rusted black iron chain, all the more appallingly alluring.

'The execution order was given just a short while ago. She was so grateful for the ending, in which she believed she finally found the ultimate meaning of her life. So she wanted to thank you again, Your Honor.'

'But I haven't been able to save her.'

'You have saved the Great Tang Empire.' The fly abruptly burst into a crazy dance, whirling around. 'And her beautiful image in the mind of the prince, too.'

Fly, fly, fly,
I'm going to die.
No need to sigh or cry,
In a peaceful shadow I lie.

Judge Dee woke up with a start, his palms sweaty with the unsuccessful effort to wave off the insistent fly fizzing in the dream. He found himself disoriented by the confusing juxtaposition of appearance and reality.

The message he had just obtained in the dream appeared to have been a true one. About her execution, Mayor Pei too had said something to that effect in the letter.

The carriage was rolling on, a bit more steadily than before. He pulled up the curtain again. The road became wider, smoother, with the distant mountains vividly verdant after the rain. White clouds unfurled in leisure against the horizon. The view looked so enchanting, as if intent on making a spendthrift offering of its beauty to a thankless world.

A small black animal was suddenly seen shooting along the gravel roadside – possibly a black fox.

He took out the copy of *Diamond Sutra* Han Shan had given him at their parting. It was conventional for people to chant Buddhist scripture for the dead, but he thought it would be too dramatic for him to do so for the moment.

Without opening the booklet, a passage at the end of the *Diamond Sutra* came flashing back to mind like the fly, and he started weeping, all of a sudden, like a young sentimental man again.

'*All the appearances of causalities in this world, therefore, are to be seen like a dream, an illusion, a bubble, a shadow, a drop of dew, or a flash of lightning.*'

POSTSCRIPT

The Shadow of the Empire is conceived as being written by Inspector Chen during *Inspector Chen and the Private Kitchen Murder*, which was also published by Severn House.

This novel is based on a real Tang Dynasty murder case, which involved a beautiful, talented, and luscious poetess Yu Xuanji (844–871). Because of the sensational, salacious details of the murder case, it has later been made into stories, movies, and TV series in China with a variety of interpretations and reinterpretations. The case was recorded only in a none too reliable, tabloid-style book titled *Little Tablets from the Three Rivers*, with scant details.

Inspired by the real historical case, Robert van Gulik wrote a *gong'an* detective novel titled *Poets and Murder* in the well-known Judge Dee series, and when the novel was published in the United States, it came out with a different title: *The Fox Magic Murder*.

In the postscript of the novel, van Gulik wrote, 'Judge Dee (Dee Renjie) was a historical person; he lived from 610 to 700 AD, and was a brilliant detective and famous statesman of the Tang dynasty. The adventures related in the present novel are entirely fictitious, however, and the other characters introduced imaginary, with the exception of the poetess Yoolan. For her I took as model the famous poetess Yu Hsuanchi [Yu Xuanji], who lived from ca. 844 to ca. 871. She was indeed a courtesan, who after a checkered career ended her life on the scaffold, accused of having beaten a maidservant to death; but the question of whether she was guilty or not has never been solved. For more details about her career and her work, the reader is referred to my book *Sexual Life in Ancient China* (E. J. Brill, Leyden, 1961), pp. 172–175. The poem quoted in the present novel was actually written by her.'

A couple of interesting points about Robert van Gulik's rendition in his *Poets and Murder* first.

Judge Dee and Empress Wu were active around the same historical period, but Xuanji wasn't until quite a number of years later. Van Gulik might not have been able to resist the temptation of putting the most well-known 'judge' and the most celebrated poetess/murderer together in one of the most sensational murder cases in the history of the Tang Dynasty.

Nor can I resist the temptation.

Also, 'Judge' and 'Magistrate' are the conventional mistranslations or misrepresentations in English regarding the Chinese official positions. In China's governmental system, there was no separation of the executive and the judicial powers. Dee Renjie, for instance, actually served in a number of high-ranking governmental positions in his prolonged official career, such as prime minister or provincial governor, exercising executive power most of the time, though from time to time he also held trials like a judge in the judicial capacity.

So it is not that accurate to call him 'Judge Dee.' At the time he exercised his judicial power, as a high-ranking government official, he had no choice but to place political interests above law and justice. As in other Judge Dee cases penned by van Gulik, particularly such *Poets and Murder*, it was a difficult job indeed for Judge Dee to serve as a judge independent of political entanglement in the background. Unfortunately, the lack of judicial independence in the Tang Dynasty remains unchanged in today's China.

In van Gulik's *Poets and Murder*, however, the Xuanji case is set in the background, and Xuanji is represented as a marginal character, coming very late into the storyline of the novel – in the midst of some other fictional murder cases Judge Dee has to deal with. A more appropriate title, therefore, should have been *Poets and Murders*.

The present novel focuses on Xuanji in the foreground with a backdrop of the real Tang Dynasty power struggle around the throne. Any reinterpretation of history cannot but be made in the present moment of history, which may perhaps demonstrate a historical paradox: China changes and China does not change through all these years.

While the poem quoted in van Gulik's novel is not in its entirety, the poems quoted fully in the appendix of this Judge Dee story were truly written by Xuanji and other Tang Dynasty poets. The importance of poetry in the Tang Empire cannot be over-exaggerated.

As often lamented, however, it is near impossible to translate the poetry. The translation can hardly do justice to the original. They were required in the story, however, given the significance of the poems to the fictional murder investigation and in their shaping of the main characters. This is even the case with Chen Cao. Inspector Chen is presented as the author of this story following *Inspector Chen and the Private Kitchen Murder*, where he has to push himself to the limit with a Confucianist quotation he learned from his late father: 'a man has to try his hand at the impossible mission' – which is also said by Judge Dee in this book.

In the first chapter of *Dream of the Red Chamber*, the novelist Cao Xueqin complains in a short poem, the last two lines of which read: 'People take the author as crazy; / who can tell the book's real flavor.' In the increasingly difficult days in the contemporary China, perhaps the same can be said of *The Shadow of the Empire*.

Inspector Chen awakes wondering
if it is he who dreamed
of being a butterfly, or if it is
a butterfly that dreams
of being Robert van Gulik,
the manuscript still smelling
of the fresh and fragrant ink
from a fox-tail brush pen
on the desk.

APPENDIX

A group of poems written by Xuanji, and by some other poets related to Xuanji, such as Wen Tingyun, Han Shan, and Wu Zetian. Needless to say, Judge Dee was also a poet, though inferior in their company. So his work is not included.

Xuanji's Poems

Willow Trees by the River
Letter to Wen Tingyun on a Winter Night
To Zi'an, Looking out across Han River in Sorrow
To Wen Tingyun
Letter to Zi'an across Han River
To a Girl in the Neighborhood
Letter to a Friend: Thoughts in the Late Spring
The Flute Sobbing
The Fading Peony
Reply to Li Ying's Letter about Angling
To Guoxiang
Farewell
Grateful Response to Court Secretary Li for His Sending over the Precious Mattress
To Li Ying on His Return from the Fishing Trip in the Summer
A Visit to the South-Overlooking Tower in Chongzhen, and to the Post of the Newly Successful Candidates in the Civil Service Examination
Boudoir Sorrow

Wen Tingyun's Poems

The Islet Enclosed in White Duckweed
Lament of the Inlaid Lute
A Green-Shaded Window
Water-Hourglass
Thousands of Woes
Fragrance from the Jade Burner

Wu Zetian's Poems

Red Promenade Skirt
The Robe to Dee Renjie with the Inscription

Han Shan's Poem

The Stars Spreading Out

Willow Trees by the River
Yu Xuanji (844–871)

> The verdant trees stretching long
> along the desolate bank, a tower distantly
> dissolving into the faint mist,
> petals falling, falling over an angler,
> with the reflection rippling
> on the autumn water,
> the old tree's root turning
> into a secluded fish-hiding spot,
> and the twigs low-hanging,
> tying a sampan –
> I'm startled out of a dream:
> the night of roaring wind and rain
> is infused with my new worries.

This is the poem Xuanji wrote at her first meeting with Wen Tingyun, a poem that instantly made her famous in the circle. In classic Chinese poetry, willow is a constantly used image suggesting love, melancholy, languidness. More often than not, those poems present lovers parting with weeping willows in the background.

Letter to Wen Tingyun on a Winter Night
Yu Xuanji (844–871)

Thinking hard, I search for the lines
to recite under the lamplight,
too nervous to spend the sleepless,
long night under the chilly quilt,
with the leaves trembling, falling
in the courtyard, fearful
of the wind coming,
and the curtain flapping
forlornly under the moon sinking . . .

Busy or not, I am always aware
of the unquenchable yearning
deep inside me. My heart remains
unchanged through the ups and downs.
The parasol tree being no place
for perching, a lone bird circles
the woods at dusk, chirping,
and chirping in vain.

Xuanji's love poems are often in the form of letters to her lovers, among whom Wen Tingyun and Zi'an (Li Yi) were also well-known poets, so they wrote poems in response to each other, as was a popular practice among Chinese literati at the time. Wen was one of the most prominent Tang Dynasty poets, and a number of his poems could have been read as his letters to her. Zi'an, the man who 'kept' Xuanji for a short period as his concubine, was a successful official but a lesser poet, and none of his love poem letters to her were passed down to later generations.

To Zi'an, Looking out across Han River in Sorrow
Yu Xuanji (844–871)

Myriads of maple leaves
upon myriads of maple leaves
silhouetted against the bridge,
a few white sails return late in the dusk.

How do I miss you?

My thoughts of you run
like the water in the West River,
flowing eastward, never-ending,
day and night.

To Wen Tingyun
Yu Xuanji (844–871)

The crickets chirruping in confusion
by the stone steps, the crystal-clear
dewdrops glistening on the tree leaves
in the mist-enveloped courtyard,
the music floating from the neighbors
under the moonlight, I look out, alone,
from the high tower to the far-away view
of the lambent mountains. The wind chilly
on the bamboo mattress, I can only express
my sadness through the decorated zither.
Alas, you are too lazy to write a letter
to me. What else can possibly come
to console me in the autumn?

Letter to Zi'an across Han River
Yu Xuanji (844–871)

The south of the river looking,
looking across to the north
of the river, sorrowfully,
in vain. We keep on missing
and thinking of those moments
of reading our lines to each
other. Inseparable mandarin ducks
nestling on the warm sandbar,
and teals flying in pairs
through the tangerine groves,
a mist-enveloped song
barely audible in the dusk,
the moon shines gloomily
on the ferry. Alas, I am so far
from you, as if stranded
at the other end of the world,
feeling all the more unbearable
with the sound of the families beating,
washing their clothes in the river.

A number of Xuanji's love poems to Zi'an present her standing by the river. While working at an official position somewhere else, Zi'an was also watched by his wife who was madly jealous of Xuanji, and he could not come down the river for her.

To a Girl in the Neighborhood
Yu Xuanji (844–871)

> You cover your face with the silk sleeves,
> bashful in the sunlight, too languid
> to apply make-up in the worries
> of the springtime. Alas, it is easier
> to find an extremely valuable treasure
> than a true-hearted lover.
> Weeping against the tear-soaked pillow
> at night, you suffer a heartbreak
> walking in the midst of the flowers.
> With a handsome talent like Song Yu
> beside you, why should you feel bitter
> about a cold-hearted Wang Chang?

In some Tang Dynasty poetry collections, the poem has another title: To Zi'an. Possibly an alternative title, which in itself speaks of her attachment to him, even in the days after he broke up with her. In the poem, Song Yu was a famous poet also known for his handsome appearance during the spring and autumn time period, and Wang Chang was another legendary good-looking but cold-hearted man in the Tang Dynasty. In classic Chinese poetry, allusion or intertextuality is frequently employed.

Letter to a Friend: Thoughts in the Late Spring
Yu Xuanji (844–871)

Startled out of the lingering dream
by the oriole's chirping, I touch
my tearful face with a light
make-up. A thin moon silhouetted
against the shady bamboo groves,
along the tranquil riverside,
the evening mist rising thick,
the swallows pecking wet soil
to build their nest, and bees flitting
among flowers for honey – alone,
I'm weighed down with all the worries,
with my self-murmuring
weighing down the pine branches.

The Flute Sobbing
(To the Tune of Yiqin'e)
Yu Xuanji (844–871)

The flute sobbing,
waking from her dream,
she sees the moon shining,
above the high tower. The moon
shining above the high tower,
the willows turn green again, year
after year, along Baling Bridge,
where lovers sadly part.

On the Cold Autumn Day
in Yueyou plateau,
no dust of a messenger rides
along the ancient path.
No dust of a messenger,
in the west wind, the sun set
against the Han royal mausoleum.

The authorship of the poem remains controversial. Some critics attribute it to Li Bai, but in terms of its style, others credit it to Xuanji.

The Fading Peony
Yu Xuanji (844–871)

So many blossoms falling,
falling in the wind, I am sighing,
with the fragrance fading,
failing in the disappearance
of yet another spring.
The peony proves to be too expensive
for the close-fisted customers,
and its sweet scent, too strong
to the flirting butterflies.
The royal palace alone deserves
such a blaze of red petals.
How can the green foliage
endure the dust and dirt
by the roadside?
Only with its transplantation
into the grand imperial garden
will those young dandies
come to regret.

Regarding the absurd political symbolism of the peony in the Tang Empire, particularly under the reign of Empress Wu, see the discussion in the section when Judge Dee first reads the poem.

Reply to Li Ying's Letter about Angling
Yu Xuanji (844–871)

> The boundless fragrance of the lotus flower
> is sweet-scenting my summer dress –
> but where are you, my lord?
> When are you coming back,
> paddling the sampan?
> What a shame we are not
> even comparable to a pair
> of mandarin ducks swimming, splashing,
> caring, cherishing, caressing
> each other around the jutting rock
> on which you sit angling.

Xuanji had a number of admirers, for whom she wrote romantic poems. Li Ying was one of those admirers, who succeeded with flying colors in the capital civil service examination in 855, and was appointed as an official. Li Ying and Xuanji were quite close. And those poems she wrote for him were suggestively salacious. In classical Chinese poetry, the image of mandarin ducks is symbolic of inseparable lovers.

To Guoxiang
Yu Xuanji (844–871)

Drunk at dusk, at dawn, I am missing
you, and the spring comes again
in the midst of my missing.
A messenger journeying through the rain,
and the solitary one standing
by the window is suffering
the heart-breaking pain.
Lifting the pearl curtain brings
the view of the distant mountains;
sadness overwhelms me again
with the green, sweet-smelling grass.
Alas, ever since our parting
at the exquisite banquet,
how many times the quiet dust
has fallen from the roof beams?

Farewell
Yu Xuanji (844–871)

During those soft, tender nights unfolding
out to my heart's content
in the towering boudoir, little did I think
my ethereal love would one day leave me.
Waking or dreaming, I care not
about where the drifting cloud
is really heading –
a fading light,
a fluttering moth.

Grateful Response to Court Secretary Li for His Sending over the Precious Mattress
Yu Xuanji (844–871)

> Spreading out the new precious bamboo mattress
> under me in the emerald tower,
> at once I feel the jade-green water rippling,
> in the depth of my heart . . .
> Alas, like the dumped silk fan
> of the deserted Han imperial concubine,
> the mattress and the fan come to bemoan
> with each other the common fate
> in the autumn's early arrival.

Court Secretary Li was none other than Li Ying. A central allusion of the poem is about Ban Jieshu (around 48 BC*), an imperial concubine in the Western Han Dynasty, who wrote about the fate of a round fan in the autumn – in subtle comparison to her fate after she was deserted by the emperor. Ezra Pound wrote a short piece in imitation of it. And the mattress in Xuanji's poem is an image in parallel: in the autumn's early arrival, it too is cast aside. Xuanji sees the resemblance between the fan and the mattress once they are no longer important to the people who have used them.*

To Li Ying on His Return from the Fishing Trip in the Summer
Yu Xuanji (844–871)

> Staying in the same lane, we have hardly met
> once through the year. Now
> you're sending an old acquaintance these cool lines,
> the osmanthus buds newly gathered
> from the sweet-scented tree.
> The Way of the nature conquering
> snow and ice, the heart of Zen
> laughing at the splendor
> of silk and satin. Treading high
> into the Milky Way, we find
> no trail connecting with
> the mist-strewn waves
> down beneath us.

A Visit to the South-Overlooking Tower in Chongzhen, and to the Post of the Newly Successful Candidates in the Civil Service Examination
Yu Xuanji (844–871)

> Amidst the cloud-mantled peaks
> the azure spring sky emerges,
> greeting the eyes around;
> all the bold, vigorous strokes
> of the characters written
> on the post appear as clear-cut
> as silver hooks. The satin dress I wear,
> alas, eclipses the shining poems
> I write. Gazing up
> at the long, long list
> of the successful candidates, I envy,
> envy them, in vain.

In ancient China, for the men of letters aspiring to success, an official career, and higher social status, the path was through the civil service examination, of which poetry-writing was an integrated part. The successful candidates were awarded government positions in accordance with their scores in the examination. The poem titles in classic Chinese poetry could be long, and this poem helps to explain why Xuanji felt so bitter about gender prejudice in the Tang Dynasty. A woman like Xuanji – in fact, all women – was barred from partaking in the civil service examination, however talented she might have been as a poetess. So she wrote the poem on the occasion of looking up at the list of new successful candidates, and she could not help feeling frustrated as an ambitious female intellectual in the Tang Dynasty.

Boudoir Sorrow
Yu Xuanji (844–871)

A full grasp of weeds, I'm weeping
against the declining light,
only to hear a neighbor's husband
returning home. Alas, the day you left,
wild geese were flying north
in the spring, and today, they are
flying south in the autumn.
Through the spring, through
the autumn, I keep missing you;
through the autumn, through
the spring, there is no message
coming to me. The windows
and doors shut, you are not here.
The noise of a wife beating,
washing her man's clothes
in the stream –
Oh, why should the sound
come through to me,
piercing the silk curtain?

The Islet Enclosed in White Duckweed
Wen Tingyun (812–870)

After applying her make-up,
she stands leaning against the balcony,
looking out to the river, alone,
to thousands of sails passing along –
none is the one she waits for.

The sun setting slant,
the water running silent, long,
her heart is breaking
at the sight of the islet enclosed
in white duckweed.

Wen Tingyun was a celebrated Tang Dynasty poet. His most successful poems are a group of love poems speaking from a female perspective. It is believed that some of his poems originated from his romantic relationship with Xuanji, imagining what she could be thinking at the moment.

Lament of the Inlaid Lute
Wen Tingyun (812–870)

Still, no dream comes to her,
the split-bamboo-made mat cool
on the silver-inlaid bed.
The deep blue skies appear like water,
the night clouds insubstantial.
The cries of the wild geese journey
as far as the Xiaoxiang River.
The moon continues shining
into her room.

A Green-Shaded Window
(To the Tune of Pusaman)
Wen Tingyun (812–870)

The bright moon, the jade tower –
the long memories . . .
The willow shoots swing so softly
in the languid spring breeze.
The weeds grown high beyond our gate
obliterated your departing figure,
but not your horse's neigh.

Against the satin valance
painted with flying golden kingfishers,
a perfumed candle dissolves in tears.
Amid withering flowers and weeping cuckoos,
appears a green-shaded window,
still lost in dream.

A considerable number of Wen Tingyun's poems are in ci form, set to specific tunes. They are not part of the titles, merely indicating something like a Petrarchan sonnet or Shakespearean sonnet in terms of versification.

Water-Hourglass
(To the Tune of Genglouzi)
Wen Tingyun (812–870)

The willow shoots long, the spring rain light,
Beyond the flowers, the water-hourglass
Drip, drop by drop –
Distantly, flushing the wild geese
at the frontier and the birds
on the ancient city wall,
but not the golden partridge
painted on the screen here.

The thin mist of the incense comes
through the embroidered curtain.
Overlooking the pond, her room is wrapped
in solitude. Against a red candle,
behind the brocade valence hung low,
her dream is long, unknown to him.

Thousands of Woes
(To the Tune of Dream of the South)
Wen Tingyun (812–870)

Thousands of woes!
And the saddest woe comes
when he chooses to stay far,
far away, at another end
of the world. The moon shining
above the mountains does not know
the worry in my heart. The breeze
rippling the water, petals keep falling
in vain. Obliquely, the azure clouds
start swaying, swaying.

Fragrance from the Jade Burner
(To the Tune of Genglouzi)
Wen Tingyun (812–870)

Fragrance from the jade burner,
tear drops from the red candles,
come reflecting her autumn thought,
stubbornly, in the superb room.
The mascara fading thin,
the cloud-like hair disheveled,
the night is so long, and the quilt,
the pillows feel chilly.
The Chinese parasol tree,
the rain tapping at midnight,
there's no telling the sadness
of separation. One leaf
after another falling,
one pattering after another
beating on the empty steps
till the arrival of dawn.

Red Promenade Skirt
Wu Zetian (624–705)

Missing you in tears, day
and night, I am so devastated,
seeing scarlet as green in a trance –
Unbelievable, I take out the red
promenade skirt from the trunk
to double-check the color.

Wu Zetian was the first empress in Chinese history. She started by serving as a palace lady – lower in status than an imperial concubine – with the first emperor of the Tang Dynasty, Emperor Taizong, who took a liking to her. After his death, she was put into a Daoist nunnery, where, even as a nun, she carried on in secret with his ninth son, Emperor Gaozong, and later married him and became his empress. The poem was said to be written in the days of her secret, difficult relationship with him, which was considered a scandal in the light of Confucianist ethics. The poem was composed during that period. With Emperor Gaozong in poor health, and then after his death, she became the de facto ruler of China, the only empress regnant in Chinese history. She ruled from 665 to 690 through her husband and sons. It was a period marked with court conspiracies. A competent ruler, she had a number of capable officials working under her, including Judge Dee.

The Robe to Dee Renjie with the Inscription
Wu Zetiàn (624–705)

> An incorruptible mainstay for the Empire
> you have worked so hard and diligently
> at the prominent official position,
> and are truly the best example
> to all your colleagues.

It was considered a great honor for an official to be given a robe, particularly with an inscription on it by the Empress Wu. Judge Dee was one really trusted by her. She was said to have broken down, weeping bitterly on Judge Dee's death, declaring, 'Now the court is empty!' Afterward, when confronted with difficult decisions, she would say, 'Why should the Old Heaven deprive me of my capable premier!'

The Stars Spreading Out
Han Shan (active in the early eighth century)

The stars spreading out, far and wide,
present a deeper, sincerer night sky.
Refusing to sink, the moon
hangs on like a solitary light burning
against the steep mountain cliff.
No need for any polishing,
the moon appears so round, bright:
suspending still in the night sky
is my very heart.